Hook

CEE BOWERMAN

BOOK TWO

Professionally edited by Chrissy Riesenberg

CEE BOWERMAN BOOK LIST

Texas Knights MC

Home Forever

Forever Family

Lucky Forever

Love Forever

Texas Kings MC

Kale

Sonny

Bird

Grunt

Lout

Smokey

Tucker

Kale & Terra (Novella)

John & Mattie

Bear

Daughtry

Hank

Fain

Grady

Stoffer

Conner Brothers Construction

Finn

Angus

Mace

Ronan

Royal

Rojo, TX

Rason & Eliza

Atlas & Addie

Jazmyne & Luc - *COMING JUNE 2021!*

Time Served MC

Boss

Hook

Chef - *COMING AUGUST 2021!*

Please follow Cee on Facebook, Instagram, and Twitter.

Also, for information on new releases and to catch up with Cee, go to www.ceebowermanbooks.com

A NOTE FROM THE AUTHOR

Dear Reader,

I'm happy to bring you the second book of the Time Served MC series. I hope you enjoy getting to know Hook and Paula, two characters who were introduced in *Boss*.

This series goes hand-in-hand with the Ciara St. James series about the Ares Infidels. You'll encounter quite a few of those characters in this book and the rest of the series.

I'd like to give a special shout out to my friend Paula. I based Hook's love interest on my friend and put in some of her quirky personality so that the readers could love her just as much as I do. She's been a great help to me while planning out so many books. I have no idea what I'd do without her. She helps me get my thoughts in order, laughs when I start getting too crazy with a storyline, and helps rein me in when I get sidetracked and don't know where my characters are headed.

Paula has become a good friend to me, and I can't imagine going a day without her sarcasm and laughter. I look forward to making her laugh so hard she chokes on whatever she's drinking and listening to her tell me 'you need Jesus' at least once in every conversation.

So, Paula, my tiny little friend from the north, if you're reading this, I just want you to know that someday when you publish your own book, I expect you to write a nice blurb at the beginning telling everyone about your big Sasquatch friend from Texas.

And it's Coke, not pop.

Cee

PROLOGUE

ONE MONTH AGO

HOOK

"Ma'am, I understand that you spent almost $1000 on this dog, but that doesn't make him immune to illness. His chart shows that he was due for his follow-up vaccinations almost a year ago. The receptionist spoke to you the first week in February, the third week in February, and again right before St. Patricks day when you told her to, and I'll quote, 'Stop fucking bothering me about this shit. The dog will be fine'. Do you remember that conversation?"

"It was to the point of harassment," the uptight woman huffed. "How was I supposed to know he really needed more shots? It sounded like a ploy for you to make more money."

"Do you have kids, ma'am?"

"No. What does that have to do with anything?"

I heard Leo, one of my techs, mutter, "Gracias a Dios." Judging from the sour expression on her face, my lovely customer also heard it and knew enough Spanish to get offended. I headed her off at the pass and put my hand up.

"There is a schedule for vaccinations that's listed on the paperwork each client is given during their first visit. The calls that you chose to ignore were reminders that you needed to bring the little guy in for the rest of the shots that would protect him from this sort of thing. You didn't follow through, and he's very sick now. Even if we do everything we can, he still might not make it."

"I'm not paying for treatment if you can't guarantee he's going to get better."

I took a deep breath and resisted the urge to pick the bitch up and throw her through the window. My friend Brea said I had a serial killer stare, and Ms. Snottybitch apparently agreed. I saw her shrink in on herself the longer I stared at her. She finally looked down at the dog on the table beside us.

"My husband has always hated my dog. He won't ever agree to pay for this." I continued to stare at her, waiting for her decision. I could see it in her eyes before she said it. She was about to give up on the sweet animal she had agreed to care for. People like her really pissed me off. She quietly asked, "When he dies, will you get rid of him for me?"

"Leo, will you take Ms. Hanson to the front and have Linda get her signature on an ownership transfer, please?"

I heard Leo grumbling under his breath and knew he was equally unhappy with the bitch. Once she was out of the room, I turned around and put my hand on the dog's side. The poor guy was so dehydrated that I was surprised he was still alive.

"Okay, buddy. We're rid of her now, and it's just me and you. I'm gonna try and make you feel better," I whispered as I thought out a game plan to save his life. We'd need to start an IV immediately. Leo walked back into the room carrying a tray of equipment along with the signed sheet of paper giving me the dog. I noticed that everything we'd need to get his treatment started was on that tray. "How did you know I was going to try and save him?"

"Same way I knew you were working hard to resist throwing that bitch out the window."

"So you're psychic then."

"I'm not psychic, Hook, but great minds think alike."

For the next hour, Leo and I worked to save the dog. He eventually started to perk up a bit, letting me know that the medicine and the fluids were doing their part. It would take quite a bit of strength for the pup to make it, and while we worked Leo and I had discussed names for the little badass.

I decided to name him Bruce after the legendary Bruce Lee. Now I just needed to find someone to take him in once he was on the mend. As I leaned against the back of the building in my hidden, shaded area next to Tonya's pen, I smoked and scrolled through my contacts. I had several people who'd let me know they'd be interested in a new dog, but most of them weren't up for one with Bruce's medical needs. My victim pool was limited, at least until he was well.

I went through my list and called potentials. I received three definite rejections, one hell no, and a maybe.

As a last resort, I decided to hit up my new friend Jenn. She had property bordering mine and was quite the animal lover. She'd 'volunteered', mostly after making me beg, to take in quite a few animals who needed a good home here recently. I almost felt guilty since just two days ago, she'd taken over care of two newborn alpacas that needed to be bottle fed every four hours.

Jenn answered on the third ring, and our conversation was short and sweet.

I hung up on her when she couldn't quit laughing.

It looked like I was the proud new owner of a four-pound teacup Yorkie. Having a dog small enough to sit in my hand was going to do wonders for my image.

PAULA

The lady next to me sighed when her phone rang and then I heard her mumble a few words before she started laughing softly. Whatever the person on the other end of the line had said was funny enough to bring tears to the woman's eyes.

I let my head fall back as the woman at my feet started my massage. It was all I could do not to moan out loud when her thumbs pressed into my arch. A woman in a chair across the room started talking loudly. I opened my eyes and saw that she was talking on the phone. I watched her for a minute, wondering if she realized that her loud conversation was disturbing everyone.

When I looked to my left, I saw the woman who had the quiet phone conversation earlier staring across the room. The look on her face was about as deadly as mine. As if she wanted to see just how far she could push us, the lady across the way hit the speakerphone button on her phone so we could hear *both* sides of the conversation.

"Really?" The woman next to me growled before she let out a loud sigh. "Some people, I swear."

"Do you think we could still hear the conversation if I shoved that phone up her ass?"

"As rewarding as that might be, I think you should shove it down her throat so she chokes on it. That way, we don't have to hear either side of the conversation."

"You have a very good point."

The two of us were quiet for a few minutes as we glared daggers at the inconsiderate woman. She realized that we were watching her and had the balls to mention it to her friend on the other end of the line. The final straw was when she laughed loudly and said, "Yeah, the old broads are getting all pissed off right about now."

"She just said that."

The woman next to me nodded and agreed, "She sure did."

"Oh, hell no," I mumbled as I gently took my foot away from the sweet woman who was tasked with my pedicure today. I put up one finger and smiled at her. She nodded and looked at me curiously. As soon as I swung my legs over the side of the foot tub, she pulled her lips between her teeth. She needed a translator 15 minutes ago when I was telling her how I wanted my toes painted, but she clearly understood the universal signs of a pissed off woman.

In my wet, bare feet, I stomped across the room and snatched the phone out of the loud bitch's hand and tossed it into the water at her feet.

"Looks like you lost the signal." I could hear the woman who'd been sitting next to me laughing just as the girl in front of me started screeching. I pointed my finger at her and growled, "If you don't shut the fuck up, I'll snap you in half and hold you under the fucking water until you're quiet. Some of us are trying to relax, goddammit!"

I calmly walked back across the room. When I stepped up next to my chair, the woman next to me was still laughing and stuck her hand up for a high five. When she'd gotten control of herself, and I was comfortable in my seat again, she stuck her hand in my direction and introduced herself. "Hi! My name is Jenn, and you're my new hero."

"Paula Clewley. It's nice to meet you."

"That bitch is going to call the police. You know that, right?"

"I can't help it if she dropped her damn phone in the water."

Jenn looked thoughtful as she stared at the crying woman. "She should be more careful. It's never a good idea to talk on the phone with a tub of water right there at your feet. Anything can happen."

"Anything."

"Have you ever seen the movie Step Brothers?"

I laughed for a second, knowing exactly where she

was going with this conversation. "I have."

"Did we just become best friends?"

"Yep."

"Do you want to go do karate in the garage?"

"Yep."

HOOK

"Anybody home?" I yelled through the screen door as I stood on my friend Brea's front porch. "If I was a criminal, I could already be inside, you know!"

Brea came around the corner with a smile on her face and her middle finger up in a universal greeting before she unlatched the screen door and stepped back so I could come in.

"If you were a decent criminal, you wouldn't show up on a bike that sounds like that."

"I obviously suck at being a criminal since I already served time in prison. But seriously, you need to be more careful, babe. There's some shit going on in town, and I don't want you and Sis to fall victim to it."

"I've seen some stuff on the news lately that did make me wonder what our little town was coming to," Brea admitted as I followed her into the kitchen. "Coffee?" When I nodded, Brea poured me a mug and passed it across the bar before she got the creamer out of the refrigerator and slid it over too. "How is the police chief I voted for?"

"You registered to vote just for Boss?"

"Of course. I wouldn't jump through those hoops for just anyone."

"I registered the day I got off paper."

Brea and I were both convicted felons, but luckily, in the state of Texas, if you were out of prison and 'off paper', meaning done with parole, you could register to vote again.

"Is Boss adjusting alright?"

"He is, but there's some shit going down, like I said, so you and Sis need to be more careful out here alone."

"I'll do better. You know Sis is a creature of habit, so she doesn't act like her mama and leave the door open for strangers."

"Is she home?"

"Not yet. She should be here anytime now. Are you going to stay for dinner?"

"I'm supposed to meet Boss, so I guess not."

"Call and invite him too. I've got plenty to go around."

"I'll call him while I smoke," I told Brea as I stood up. I picked up my mug and took it outside where I settled into the porch swing as I called Boss. He picked up, and we talked for a minute. He was more than happy to come over to have some home cooked food for a change. I'd just lit my cigarette when a car pulled up in the driveway. Sis, Brea's daughter, got out and walked toward the house. "Hi, sweetheart!"

"Hi, Hook."

"How was work today?"

15

"Pop was on a tear, so I hid myself away and did inventory most of the day."

"What was he on a tear about?"

"Soda and I did something different that came close to pulling the business into this century. You know how the man hates change."

"Well, I may have something that can bring a smile to your face," I told the young woman as she sat down next to me on the swing. She didn't say anything, just stared at me with her normal expression. I unsnapped the top few fastenings on my cut and reached into the pocket where I'd stashed her gift. I pulled him out and let him settle on my hand as I watched her jaw drop and her eyes get wide. "This is Bruce."

"Bruce?" Sis whispered as she reached out and took the little dog. She snuggled him up against her chin and his tiny tongue darted out and licked her. "Holy shit, Hook. He's so cute!"

"Isn't he, though?"

"And he's so little!"

"That's as big as he's going to get. He's a little over a year old now."

"And you just carry him around in your pocket?"

"I have been for the last few weeks. The little guy was so sick that he almost didn't make it. I've been nursing him back to health. I need to find him a good home where he'll be cared for with people I can trust." Sis turned her head and stared at me with a wicked gleam in her eye. She knew just what I was saying. This wasn't the first time I'd brought them a pet to love. "I thought he'd get along with the rest of your brood."

"Does Mom know?"

"Nope. I'm not giving him to your mom. I'm giving him to you."

"Oh, you're in so much trouble, buddy. You know that's why you're my very favorite, right? Let's play a trick on Mom!"

"I'm in. What are we doing?"

Sis reached down and picked up the large steel travel mug she'd carried with her onto the porch. She handed it to me, and I took the lid off and saw it was empty. She gently put Bruce down inside and gave him a little kiss before she took it from me and walked toward the house. As I followed her in, I realized I couldn't see the dog inside the mug, and I knew just what she was about to do.

"Mom!" Sis yelled as she walked into the house.

"What?" Brea yelled from the kitchen where I'd left her a few minutes ago.

"You've got to taste this!"

I came around the corner just in time to see Sis hand the cup to a distracted Brea who was looking down at the chopping board in front of her. Brea glanced at her daughter and over at me before she leaned toward Sis for a sip. Sis tipped the cup just a bit, and Brea looked down into it and squealed with excitement.

I sat down at the bar and sipped my coffee as I watched the two women fall in love with their new pet. They were still all aflutter when Boss showed up. I laughed when they handed him the little dog. His usually stern face melted into awe just like Brea's had, and I watched my friend study the tiny dog.

"Where do you get animals like this, man?" Boss asked as he snuggled the dog up close to his neck.

Over dinner, I told my friends about the previous owner and how easily she'd given up on her pet. They were just as appalled as I was about it.

"You should have thrown her out the window, and let Tonya play with her." Sis had used a scarf to fashion a sling for Bruce and held him close through dinner. I watched as she absentmindedly patted the dog between bites and knew I'd found him the perfect home.

"The woman was too bony. Tonya wouldn't have liked her much."

"She sounds like a bitch. I bet she would have tasted bad anyway," Brea added. "There's this woman in the office at work that I'd like to feed to Tonya."

"Here we go," Sis grumbled as she rolled her eyes at her mom. "I'm going to take Bruce and introduce him to Jewel and Toot. Thanks again, Hook."

"Of course, sweetheart. Thank you for taking him."

The three of us watched Sis go out the back door to

her small house that was in the corner of Brea's large backyard.

"You started working in an office again?" Boss asked Brea.

"It's just temp work. I was going stir crazy being here alone all day."

I chuckled and asked her, "Doing the books for me and Pop isn't enough?"

"It's one, maybe two days a week to take care of both of y'all. That leaves five days for me to fill up."

"I might be able to find a spot for you at the station . . ."

"You want me to work at the cop shop? That's just comical, Boss."

"I can hire anyone I want in the office. Your record doesn't matter at all."

"You could come and work for me a few days a week if you want. I know that Linda would appreciate the company." Brea tilted her head and looked at me as she considered my offer. "If you want to get out of the house, just come over and hang out at the clinic. There's always a litter of kittens that need to be held and dogs that need some love. The six of us can only do so much in a day, and sometimes stuff like that falls to the wayside."

"I could be a professional puppy snuggler."

Boss smiled at her and said, "I think the title suits you since you're just so fucking sweet and all."

Brea gave him a shitty look and before she said, "I'll come by and find something to do."

"While you're there, will you pretend that you and I are dating so Linda will get off my ass?"

"The thought of dating you is too repulsive. I can't."

Boss choked on the sip of beer he'd just taken and started coughing while I just stared at our friend.

"Repulsive?"

"You're like a brother or something. So gross," Brea said with a shudder. "I couldn't even pretend."

"What about me?" Boss asked her once he'd managed to catch his breath.

"Same. Y'all are gross."

"She's fucking great for our egos. Aren't you glad she's our friend?" I asked Boss sarcastically.

"If I'm so repulsive, I guess you don't want me to fix any of those tickets you're so fond of getting."

"You're not nearly as repulsive as Hook," Brea backtracked. "In the right light, you're downright handsome, Boss."

"I was going to invite you to the winter festival with me and Pop tonight, but you probably don't want to be seen with me anyway. I can't believe you. I give you free healthcare for your animals, and I'm repulsive; he offers to fix a ticket, and all of a sudden, he's handsome. That's fucked up, Brea."

"That's the reality of family, Hook. Get used to it. I can't go tonight anyway. Sis and I have a date to watch RuPaul's Drag Race."

"You can't set the DVR to record it and come with us?" Boss asked her.

"And go out around people on purpose? Uh, no."

Considering that most of the time, I felt the same way about socializing, I couldn't really argue, but I had to ask, "As family shouldn't we be dragging you out and about to socialize and meet new people?"

"I met plenty of new people when I was a guest of the state, Hook. I think I've hit my quota."

"Both of you need to find a good woman to warm your bed when you're home," Pop preached to us as Boss and I walked around the park aimlessly looking at the different booths that were set up for the winter festival while we waited for the live music to start. "I'm beginning to worry about some of you boys."

Our mentor, affectionately known by almost everyone as Pop, was back on his soapbox about how me, Boss, and our club brother Captain needed the love of a good woman. He still considered us boys even though we were creeping up toward 50. Of course, he didn't mention that he'd been single since his wife died years and years ago.

Years ago, Pop's son had gone crossways with the law

and ended up in prison. He served his time and got out only to come home to a town that didn't want him. Without a job, he had no way to afford a place of his own or anything that a man needed to make his way in life. Pop helped as much as his son would let him, but his son fell back in with the wrong crowd and ended up right back in prison where he eventually died.

Pop decided to do something to honor his son's memory and started sponsoring convicts that he thought had a good chance out in the real world if only they had some help adjusting. Over the years, he'd provided housing and employment along with encouragement and support to countless men and women. His success rate was high. Boss, Captain, Brea, and myself were just a few of the people he'd helped. There were many more, and every single one of us had an undying loyalty to Pop and considered him a father figure we couldn't live without.

Even when he meddled in our lives like he was doing right now.

"My bed is plenty warm," I told him. "My life is nice and calm too. I don't need some woman coming in and mucking everything up with drama."

"I've got enough shit on my plate now that you and your cronies got me elected to the chief of police position. Thanks to your bright idea, I don't have time for a woman."

"Boss, when the right woman comes along, you'll make time. As for you, Hook . . . sleeping in bed with your fucking cat isn't what I mean by keeping your bed warm unless you're doing some things there that are more fucked up than I'd like to consider."

"Why do all of you make jokes about that shit? You're all fucking disgusting."

"I need some good coffee to ward off this chill. There's a beauty that runs that coffee truck over there. Just looking at her will get the three of us warm all over, but when you taste the goodies she bakes, the two of you just might fight over who gets to woo her."

"Not fighting over a woman, Pop," Boss told him. "Haven't seen one yet that will knock my socks off like that."

"You just wait, son. You just wait. Let's go over there so I can prove you wrong, and you can buy this old man some coffee."

PAULA

"How's Mama feeling today?" I asked my older brother Vincente.

"She's better. The doctor gave her some antibiotics for the sinus infection. He said it probably started with allergies and she let herself get run down."

"She still won't take her allergy medication? That woman is nothing if not stubborn."

"Gina found some local honey like you suggested and has got her taking a spoon of it with her vitamins in the morning. We'll see if that helps at all."

"Can't hurt," I told my brother as I hit the speaker button and laid the phone down so I could start putting return address stickers on the box of envelopes that had just arrived in the mail. "And how is Zach?"

"He's still a cocky little shit. He's started running errands for Papa, so he's getting barked at day and night, but he seems to be handling it okay."

"Just errands?"

"Yes, Paola, just errands. Same as my kids. I swear, you and Gina share a brain or something."

"No, big brother, your wife *has* a brain. That's what confuses you."

"Whatever. There's no doubt he's your son with that mouth you've got. Oh, and he's started running with a new crowd."

"A new *good* crowd?"

"Well, an old one, but they're okay. He's been hanging out with the Rabono twins."

"And? Oh! Aren't those the boys whose father . . ."

"Their biological father killed Uncle Sal."

"Everyone's okay with that?" I asked my brother, amazed at the world I'd come from. I'd been away long enough that it seemed foreign to me now.

"You know how it is. Let bygones be bygones. Uncle Sal deserved it for what he did, and the children don't pay for the sins of the parents anyway."

I snorted at that comment but didn't argue. "Did you get my package for Iris? Hold onto it until her birthday, okay?"

"It's locked in my office. Your niece is a nosy little girl, and she can't stand to wait for her gifts. Reminds me of you when we were children."

"My niece graduated from girl to woman when she turned 25 last year and graduated at the top of her class in business school, caveman. Any trips planned in my direction soon?"

"In a month, Antonio and I have a five-hour layover at DFW. I'm sure we'll need to eat if you want to hang out."

"Text me the details. I'll make sure I'm in Dallas so you can buy me dinner."

"Of course. I have to get ready for a meeting, baby sister. Do you need anything?"

"Nope, I'm set. Love you."

"I love you too. We'll talk at our usual time next week?"

"Of course. Give kisses for me."

"Always."

I sighed after my brother hung up. We had a longstanding weekly appointment to talk on the phone so that we could check in with each other. When I was disowned by my parents and forced to move away, my weekly talks with my brothers were the only bright spots in my life.

I'd given my life to my family, and in return, I had a beautiful, stubborn son who wasn't allowed to speak to me. Luckily, since he was so stubborn, he didn't always follow the rules. I had a weekly phone call with him too.

My family was crazy, but I wouldn't trade anything for them. Well, I wouldn't trade anything for *most* of them.

Once I was finished with the envelopes, I checked my email for any new orders. There were three, and luckily, I had everything in stock. Once I'd filled the orders with the jewelry the customers had requested, I adjusted my inventory numbers in the correct spreadsheet and shut the computer down.

I'd reserved a space at the winter festival tonight and needed to go to the park and get set up. I had my Expedition loaded already, but I wanted to get there early so I could talk to Jenn for a few minutes.

My new friend and I got along very well, and I was glad. I'd been in Tenillo for years and had made some acquaintances, but not any true friends. I felt like Jenn and I could become really close. She somehow seemed to be on my frequency.

It was hard to meet new people at my age unless I was willing to join some sort of group. I wasn't the type to go to church often enough to meet anyone there. Hell, I wasn't sure that the type of people who went to church regularly would understand my sense of humor, and besides, they'd probably be curious about my past.

I did have one friend in Tenillo who knew almost everything about me. I'd known her since we were children and had even gone to college with her after I was married. Frankie Romano was a trauma surgeon who'd moved to Tenillo years ago to run the surgical team at the Amasee County Hospital. She'd heard what was going on with me through her family back home and encouraged me to move to Tenillo so I could be nearby.

My life had changed so drastically after I'd left my husband that I didn't have anyone at home to lean on. When my father's edict came down that I was no longer part of the family and not welcome anywhere in New York, I'd had no idea where I would go. Frankie's phone call rescued me. Within just a few days, I was living at her house in Tenillo and reeling from the loss of my family and my life at home.

Frankie had been gently supportive until I was ready to join the outside world again and then she'd encouraged me to start a business selling the crafts that I enjoyed making. I knew that she'd only done that so I'd get up and around, but it had turned into quite a profitable business. I needed something to focus on, and selling my crafts and making custom orders was just that. It was an excellent diversion that took my mind off of all I'd lost.

I'd slowly built my business up so that I had plenty of online orders. When I bought my house, I'd chosen it because there was plenty of room for me to house my crafts and there was a guest room just in case someone from my family came to visit.

My son was able to arrange a trip at least once a year, and my older brothers showed up randomly. Occasionally, one of my sister-in-laws would drop in, and sometimes, one of my nieces and nephews would show up and visit on their way to wherever they were headed.

My father knew that the family talked to me - he couldn't fight them all. Instead, he ignored their insubordination just like he ignored me, his only daughter. After seven years, I had come to accept that neither of my parents would ever speak to me again. And honestly, since I was a mother myself, it made me even more angry that my own parents could abandon me.

There was no way in hell I'd ever give up on my son. I'd endured marriage to his father until he was 18 just so that no one could take him away from me. I was the lamb led to the slaughter at barely 18. I should have known then that my parents, especially my father, saw me as a pawn rather than an important part of the family.

I shook off my maudlin thoughts and locked up the house so I could leave. Once I'd checked the windows and put my security in place, I set the alarm on the panel by the front door and walked out into the late afternoon sunshine. I climbed up into my Expedition and headed toward the park, ready for a delicious coffee and some baked goods from my friend Jenn's food truck.

Once I was at the park, I locked my wares in my truck and walked through the park until I found Jenn's spot. The front window wasn't open, so I walked around to the back of the truck and knocked on the door. She opened it quickly and invited me inside.

"Hey! You're early."

"I told you I'd come by," I reminded her. "I'm not set up yet, so I can't stay long."

"I've got everything ready for the most part, so I'll take a break and chat with you until you have to go."

"How are things?"

"Well, I haven't been sleeping much, and that's about to kill me."

"Are the little ones still waking you up every four hours?"

"God, yes," Jenn said with a long sigh as she mixed my favorite coffee drink. "Just a few more months, and they'll be sleeping through the night. Hook said that their weight is right on track, so I'm doing everything right. I just want a full night's rest right now."

"I could babysit," I offered without thinking. Jenn had taken in two alpaca babies a few weeks ago, and they needed to be bottle fed every four hours. I remembered when my son was that small, and I was exhausted from getting up with him every night. Once a week, my sister-in-law Gina or my other sister-in-law Maria would come over to my house and spend the night to take care of Zacharia so I could get a full night's sleep. I don't think I would have survived motherhood without their help, so I thought I should offer Jenn that same shoulder to lean on. "Pick a night that's good for both of us, and bring them over."

"You'd do that?"

"I would. New moms need a break now and then, you know."

"Oh, I almost forgot to ask. Any word from your lawyer about the phone thing?"

"He said it's an open and shut case. There weren't any fingerprints, no security video, and it's our word against hers. Somehow, all the women who were working in the salon that day have moved on with no forwarding information, so there's no way for her to call them as witnesses."

"Real unfortunate how she fumbled that phone and plopped it right into the tub."

I laughed at Jenn's obvious lie and told her, "We should know in the next week or so if the DA is going to pursue the case or not. After that, she could always sue me in civil court."

"Think she learned her lesson about being a rude little bitch?"

"Women like that never learn. The world is their oyster, don't you know?"

"Idiots. I kind of wish I had it on video, though. Might be fun to watch the look on her face over and over again."

"Losing my temper like that is why it's best if I'm only exposed to the public in small increments," I told Jenn before I took a sip of the coffee creation she'd made me. "God, this is good."

"That's the Turtle recipe I told you about. Is there too much caramel?"

"Is there such a thing as too much caramel?"

"Okay, so that's a no." Jenn laughed and took a sip of her own coffee. "Do you think we'll be busy tonight?"

"You will, for sure. There are already people mingling outside your trailer waiting for you to open."

"I hope I baked enough goodies. Oh, let me grab you a plate so you can nibble between customers."

"I'm so glad we're friends, but I'm going to be cussing you when I can only fit into my stretchy pants."

"Stretchy pants and leggings are my favorite wardrobe items," Jenn explained as she filled a styrofoam container with sweets and baked goodness for me to take with me. I knew without a doubt that she'd refuse to let me pay, but I'd already figured out what I was going to do. I reached into my pocket and handed Jenn a plastic baggie and watched her face light up when she lifted it up and looked at the pendant I'd made for her. "Oh, that's so pretty!"

"I thought you might like that. Do you have a chain it can go on? If not, I've got . . ."

"This is too much! Let me give you some money."

"It's a trade. Your deliciousness for my jewelry. At the rate we're going, I'm going to need those stretchy pants ASAP, and you're going to need a new jewelry box."

"It's worth the trade!" Jenn handed the styrofoam container to me and asked, "Do you want me to come help you set up?"

"I'm good. I've got it down to a science at this point. I wouldn't know what to do with help. Speaking of, I need to get going. I'll try and come see you later."

"I'll be here. And thank you for the pretty."

"The pretty. I like that. I'll see you later!"

I walked out of the trailer and into the fading light of the day, squinting my eyes after being inside the darker interior where Jenn was working. Once I was back in my truck, I jumped the curb and drove over the grass to the spot that was reserved for me and unpacked my tables and tent. When I was finished, I asked one of the other vendors I recognized to watch my things while I parked at the edge of the park. When I got back to my space, I put the coffee and snacks to the side and got everything set up just the way I liked it. I was ready to dazzle the citizens of Tenillo with my wares.

"Do you ship things for your customers?"

"Of course," I answered the customer who was standing off to the side behind some people who were browsing. "I can ship anywhere in the US for a nominal fee, but international shipping is quite a bit more expensive."

"Let's say I wanted to send a gift to someone along with what I buy from you. Could I come to your office and add my gift to the package you're going to send for me?"

I thought that was a strange request, but I didn't really see the harm in it until I glanced up at the customer's face. There was something about him that made me uncomfortable, and I instantly knew I didn't want him to know anything about me, especially where I lived.

"No, I don't really work that way. I can ship out the gift and you can send yours separately, or I can meet you somewhere in town and give your order to you so you can add it to your own package."

"That's not how I want to do it," the man said softly. "I want to send it with your label, not mine."

"Why?" I asked him directly as I stared him right in the eye. "That sounds a little shady."

Something flickered in his eyes, and it was all I could do not to flinch. I glanced around to see if there was anyone I knew nearby and realized that I was all alone with this man. The closest people were at the booth three spots away. The women on either side of me were elderly and wouldn't be any help if I was in danger.

"I think that if you're a good businesswoman, you'll hear me out when I bring you an offer," the man said as he picked up one of my business cards from the table. "I'd like you to think about what I've asked. I think that we could form a partnership, you and I."

"Not happening, bud," I told him as I plucked the business card out of his hands. "Move along."

He stared at me for a few seconds, and his eyes glittered with evil as he smiled at me and winked. "I don't need the card, honey. I'll be in touch."

I watched the man walk away and then picked up my phone and opened the camera app, waiting for him to pause at another booth to talk to the vendor. Once he was still, I zoomed in and took a few pictures of him before I went to my notes app and typed in everything I could remember about our conversation.

I had no idea why I felt like the details of what had just happened were so important, but I felt an unexplainable need to get everything down before I forgot even the smallest little thing. That man was going to be trouble, but he had no idea just who he was messing with.

PAULA

"I can't believe your ex-husband thought he could just show up at your house. Did he think you'd invite him in for a fucking cup of coffee? What a dick."

Jenn snorted and rolled her eyes. "He *is* a dick. I can't believe I stayed married to him all those years."

"How are you feeling? Have you had to go back to the chiropractor after your Superwoman stunt a few weeks ago?" Jenn had been approached by a sleazy asshole at one of the craft fairs, and when he'd boxed her inside her truck with no way to escape out of the door, she'd taken a dive out of the front window and landed flat on her back. I'd met her boyfriend Boss that day and realized that he was just as handsome as the men I'd met on her porch a few hours ago when her ex-husband showed up to start shit.

"I'm okay," Jenn said as she handed me the beaters she'd used to mix her latest batch of brownies to sell at an event tonight. I watched her hop up onto the counter and use the spatula to scrape some batter out of the bowl so she could have a taste too. "Have you heard from the weirdo that approached you the other day?"

"No, thank God."

"What do you think he wanted to mail?"

"From the vibe I got, I'd guess drugs. And I'd be left holding the bag if he sent it in my package with my shipping information, and the person on the other end got busted."

"That sounds like a pretty elaborate scheme for some petty drug dealer."

"He didn't give off the 'petty drug dealer' vibe. He seemed more like a crime boss or something."

"And we've got so many of those in Tenillo, huh?"

"More than you'd think, I'm sure."

Jenn and I heard a sound from inside the house and looked over at the open door of Jenn's commercial kitchen. We could only see a portion of her regular kitchen from here.

"What the hell was that?" Jenn murmured as she set her bowl aside and started to get down.

"I'll check. I need a glass of milk anyway," I told her as I slid off the stool and tossed the beaters into the sink. I walked into the house and looked around before I stepped into the kitchen. I could hear movement to my left through the doorway that led onto the covered back porch and figured that one of her many animals had escaped their confines and was rooting around looking for trouble. I walked out into the room and glanced to my right just before I felt movement on my left. Growing up with two big brothers and about a million cousins who liked to play tricks on each other had given me great reflexes.

I dodged the fist that was coming toward my face and instinctually bent forward and threw myself toward my attacker. I heard a loud 'oof' from him just as we fell to the floor. I was on top of him and pushed myself up just as I started to yell for Jenn. The man could see what I was about to do and grabbed my chin.

His hand was close to my mouth, so I turned my head and bit the shit out of him, holding onto his finger with my teeth as he pushed me to the side. He tried to yank his hand away, but I held on as I reached up and scraped my nails down his cheeks. He pulled his other hand back to hit me, and I dodged it before I pushed up with my hips and knocked him over again. Once I was on top of him with his fingers still between my teeth, I reared back and punched him twice in the face. On my third downward strike, he moved his head, and I punched the concrete next to his ear.

Pain shot up my arm, and I let his fingers go just as his other hand socked me in the face. My world went black.

When I came to, I jumped up and looked around. The man and I had trashed the patio during our scuffle. I ignored the damage we'd done and rushed into the house to check on Jenn. As I hurried past the kitchen counters, I pulled a butcher knife out of the block and rushed into the other kitchen where we'd been.

The sight in front of me stopped me short. I stood there holding the knife and I watched as my friend wielded a giant pan that she brought down on our attacker's head.

"Paula!" Jenn yelled.

"I'm here," I told her and realized that my voice sounded strange. I reached up and touched blood on my face before I moved my fingers up closer to my eye and felt the swelling.

"Are you okay? Are you alone?" Jenn asked as she propped the door to her walk-in refrigerator open with a huge bag of pecans.

"That man knocked me out."

Jenn looked at me and roared, "Fuck!" before she pulled her leg back and kicked the asshole again.

"Holy shit! You beat his ass!"

"I might have killed him," Jenn admitted calmly as we stared down at the man on the floor.

I don't think Jenn realized just how crazy the things we did over the next few minutes were, but I knew the second she'd suggested we tie him up and drag him into the walk-in rather than call the police that I'd found a woman after my own heart. Where I came from, a person didn't involve the police unless you absolutely had no other choice. Now considering Jenn's boyfriend was the chief, that might prove to be an issue here, but I didn't care. The man had broken into my friend's house and assaulted both of us.

He needed to die a horrible death and then get picked apart by some hungry fish in a body of water somewhere as far as I was concerned.

We were sitting there discussing the merits of keeping the man tied up in the refrigerator and using a temporary insanity defense when the doorbell rang. Jenn and I looked at each other with wide eyes as we scrambled to get off the floor where we were propped against the door of the walk-in.

We walked out into the kitchen and stopped when we heard a man's voice behind us. I spun around and saw a man who was so good-looking, my mouth dropped open in shock. I'd joked with Jenn that the men who'd come to save us from her ex-husband earlier were handsome, but this man took the cake.

He was much taller than me, of course, and his shoulders were so wide I knew I wouldn't be able to put my arms around him if I tried. The wide shoulders tapered down to a smaller waist and a pair of jeans that were molded to his huge thighs. I took a second to let my gaze linger below the waist of his jeans and knew there was something there that I really needed to get my hands and mouth around.

"What the fuck happened here?" the man yelled as he rushed toward us.

"Nothing," the two of us said in unison.

He skidded to a halt and studied us for a minute, confused.

"Hook, this is my friend Paula. Paula, this is Dr. York, but he likes to be called Hook. It's a motorcycle club thing, although I don't know how their names were decided." Jenn rambled, and I knew her mind had to be spinning out of control just like mine was right now.

"It's a pleasure to meet you, Hook." I took pity on Jenn and interrupted her rambling explanation and stuck my hand out to introduce myself.

Hook looked down at my hand and up at my face before he asked, "What the fuck happened to your face?" He glanced over at Jenn and asked, "And yours? Did you two get into a fist fight? Who broke the window back there? What the fuck is going on?"

I spun around and looked at Jenn before I pointed at my face and asked, "Does it really look that bad?"

"There's some blood," Jenn pointed at her own face and swirled her finger around her mouth and up her cheek. "It's kind of smeared a little bit, and your eye is swollen. Do I have blood too?"

"No, no blood," I assured her. "You need an ice pack, though. Your eye is swelling. I think mine is too. My whole face hurts now."

"So does mine."

"What. The. Fuck. Is. Going. On?" Hook had apparently lost his shock and curiosity and gone straight to anger. "Did your ex get into the house? I thought the guys were coming over. I got here as soon as I could. Where the fuck is he?"

Jenn was taking too long to explain so I jumped in. "The ex didn't get inside. Your friends came and scared the shit out of him before they chased him back to town. I was helping Jenn in the kitchen and we, um, got dizzy from the, um, oven fumes, and we accidentally bumped heads."

"We're fine, though. It's okay. You can go home and take care of your animals. We'll put some ice on our faces and be fine. I'll have Boss call you when he gets here."

Hook was looking at Jenn when the three of us heard the man in the refrigerator scream for help. Hook's eyes got wide and so did Jenn's when I said, "Man, my stomach makes some weird noises when I'm hungry. It was nice to meet you, Mr. Hook! I'm sure I'll see you again soon."

While I was talking, I took the opportunity to touch the fine specimen of man in front of me. I put my hand on Hook's bicep and tried to turn him back toward the door. He was a huge man, at least twice my size, and he didn't budge no matter how hard I tried to push him.

Instead, he looked down at me with a glare. "Your hungry stomach sounds like a full-grown man screaming for help?"

"Did it sound like that to you?" I asked Jenn with an exaggerated shrug. When the man screamed again, I closed my eyes and bit my lip before I blew out a long breath.

With a laugh that sounded more like hysteria than humor, Jenn said, "There it was again."

Hook glanced down at his arm where I was still trying to move him and reached down with his other arm to pull his phone out of his pocket. With one thumb, ignoring me as I grunted with the effort, pissed off since I couldn't even gain an inch, he pushed at the screen, and I heard Boss's voice come over the speaker.

"Did you make it?" Boss asked immediately.

"Yeah. I'm here. Are you close?" Hook answered.

"What's wrong?"

"There's a little, tiny woman here who's so hungry that her stomach is making weird noises. She and Cool Cat seem to have lost their fucking minds. I don't know if they're drunk as fuck or high as kites, but I think I need backup. So, are you close?"

"I'm pulling into the driveway now."

"Come through the back door so you can get the same view I got when I came inside."

"What the fuck?" Boss asked, exasperated.

"You're gonna say that more than once in the next few minutes, I'm sure."

The phone beeped when Boss hung up, and as Hook put it back into his pocket, Jenn sighed dramatically. As if he was tired of me wasting my effort, Hook growled, "Stop it!" and put his free arm around me and pulled me tight to his chest. I made an oof noise when I hit the brick wall that was Hook's chest and took my hand off his bicep and touched his abs before it drifted around his hip to his back.

Just as Boss walked into the kitchen, the man in the walk-in screamed for help again. Boss's face went from shock at the state of the back room to anger when he saw the bruises on Jenn's face. He slowly turned his head toward the door leading out to the commercial kitchen where the man's constant screaming had just started.

"What. The. Fuck?" Boss whispered as he turned his head back to look at Jenn.

"There's one," Hook mumbled as his other arm went around me.

"I have a question, and before we go any further with this whole screaming man thing, I need you to answer me," Jenn told her boyfriend.

"Okay," Boss drawled.

"Are you here as the chief of police or as my boyfriend?"

Boss studied her for a second and asked, "Which one do you want here?"

"The boyfriend?"

"You sure?"

"In a perfect world, Hook wouldn't have shown up, and you'd still be in your meeting so Paula and I could take some time to figure out what we're fucking doing. Since it's not a perfect world, you're both here. Obviously, that sound is not coming from her hungry stomach. We'll have to explain what happened."

"Is whoever's making that sound why your face is fucking bruised and your eye is swollen?" Boss asked.

"Same with hers," Hook told Boss as he put his hands on my shoulders and pushed me back far enough for Boss to see my face. Once Boss had a good look at my face, Hook pulled me back into his chest, and I let out another 'oof' when I hit.

"That would be a yes," Jenn answered him.

Boss took a deep breath and looked in the direction the screaming was coming from before he asked, "Is he dying?"

"No. Maybe. I'm not sure. The guy's pretty fucked up and probably needs a doctor."

Boss thought about Jenn's answer for a second before he asked, "Do you want him to get to a doctor, or do you want

43

him to be dying?"

"I want him to not be able to break into my house and hurt me and my friend again. If him dying is the way to assure that, then no, I do not want him to get medical attention, and yes, I'd like for him to be dying."

"I vote for the dying thing, and I have a few ideas on how to do it if you need input," I said from my comfortable spot in Hook's muscular arms. "I know we just met, but if the three of you knew anything at all about me, you'd understand that I'm really okay with this. I can even help."

"Want to get married?" Hook asked as he gently patted me on the back.

"Sure. I'm free next Friday."

"They've been down there quite a while," Jenn fretted as she glanced toward the back door. "I bet they're hungry."

I stared at her in shock for a second before I agreed. I sat there with an ice pack over my hand and held another one up against my face as I watched Jenn pack a huge box full of sandwiches, chips, bottled water, and fresh brownies for dessert. The two of us didn't say much, and I was okay with that as my mind raced, wondering what the men were doing in the wellhouse in the back of Jenn's property.

Things were a little different here in Texas, but what had gone on this afternoon all boiled down to the same thing

I'd seen happen with my family at home. Someone had messed with the wrong people, and he was paying for it, and probably with more pain than the human body was meant to withstand.

I was perfectly okay with that, and it seemed like Jenn was too.

The rest of the afternoon passed quickly, and finally, I was so exhausted that I couldn't keep my eyes open. Jenn made up the guest bedroom for me, and I went and laid down when she went upstairs. We'd only occasionally seen one of the men from her boyfriend's club, and I hadn't seen Hook again since I'd helped him and Boss get the man out of the walk-in and to the well house.

One of the men who'd shown up wearing a leather vest like Boss's was named Captain, and I could tell within seconds that he was a lawyer. He'd made sure that Jenn and I understood the importance of complete secrecy regarding today's events, and he'd even gone so far as to threaten us with prosecution alongside the men. I wasn't stupid. I'd noticed that Captain made sure that mine and Jenn's fingerprints were on all sorts of things that could be used against us if this ever came to trial.

Another man introduced as Stamp, who looked alarmingly like a man I'd grown up with, had come in with a bag from the hardware store and asked us to look through the items he'd purchased. Captain had watched as Jenn innocently pawed through the bag, but my sarcasm jumped to the forefront when Captain passed the bag my way.

"Want me to lick something so you have my DNA to go with my prints?" I asked him with an irritated glance. He shrugged and just to be a smartass, I licked my fingertip and touched it to the very bottom of the butane bottle where it was unlikely anyone else would touch.

Captain and another one of the men, Preacher, watched me closely as I touched the rest of the items in the bag before I pushed it back across the table toward Stamp. I knew they were worried I'd rat them out and were making sure I was just as implicated as they were.

I had to remind myself that these men had no idea who I was or where I'd come from, which meant that they had no idea how easy it would be for me to disappear and change my identity, leaving them twisting in the wind while I roamed free in another country.

Hell, the name I was using *now* wasn't even mine. It wouldn't be a problem for me to get a new one. All it would take was one phone call, and I'd have a new identity and a ride to the destination of my choice. I wouldn't be the first person in my family to disappear, that was for damn sure. I'd already done it once, after all.

I must have fallen asleep at some point because I woke up when someone gently moved my hair away from my face. I opened my eyes and stared into Hook's as he bent over the bed and studied my swollen eye.

"Are you okay, little one?"

"I didn't want to cause any drama because I knew you guys were busy, but I need to go to the ER for an x-ray, if you don't mind giving me a ride."

"What's wrong?"

"I think I have a boxer's fracture from when the man moved and I accidentally punched the concrete."

"Are you fucking kidding me?"

"No. Why would I joke about that?"

"You've been in here for hours with a broken hand?"

"Everyone was busy, and I didn't want to show up at the hospital with Jenn in tow since the two of us looked like we pissed off Ronda Rousey. My friend is on duty right now, and she can get me in under the radar if you don't mind taking me to the county hospital. If you'll just drop me off, she can take me home when her shift is over."

"You're a mystery, little one. A total fucking mystery."

4

HOOK

"Aren't you going to give her something for the pain?" I asked the doctor who was inspecting Paula's face. Paula quickly shook her head but kept her eyes closed as she concentrated on breathing through the pain the doctor was causing.

"We'll skip the narcotics tonight, I think," the doctor mumbled. I saw her wince at the same time Paula did when she touched the bridge of Paula's nose. She mumbled something close to Paula's ear. I knew it wasn't English, but couldn't hear her well enough to figure out the language. When Paula shook her head again, the doctor leaned back and said, "I don't think your nose is broken, piccola, but your hand is another story."

"I could have told you that without the x-ray," Paula mumbled, obviously in a lot of pain.

"Maybe we should get a doctor in here who doesn't have a problem tossing out pain medication," I growled as I stood up to walk toward the door.

"Hook, she'd give them to me if I asked," Paula assured me as she opened her eyes and looked at me. I stopped in the doorway and stared at her for a minute before I walked back over and sat in the chair I'd moved close to the exam table.

"If she really needs them, I can take her to my house and let her sleep there where she's safe," the doctor assured me, but it just confused me even more.

"You think I'm a danger to her?" I was pissed now, but I couldn't really blame either woman. Paula had just met me this afternoon, and the doctor didn't even know my damn name.

"That's not what she means. If I'm going to take anything more than Tylenol, I need to make sure I'm around someone who I can trust with any secrets the drugs might make me spill. I just met you, but I've known Frankie since I was a kid. There's not much about me that she doesn't already know."

"Are you in witness protection or something?" I asked her. Both of the women laughed at my question, but neither of them denied it. Frankie leaned close to Paula's ear and whispered something else I couldn't understand. Paula answered her and I could tell it was in another language again.

"I'm not in witness protection, Hook. You don't have to wait for me. Once Frankie gets done putting on my cast, I can wait in her car until she gets off work. She'll take me back to her place, and I can stay there for a while.

I'd spoken to Preacher and Captain before I woke Paula up at Jenn's house, and the three of us had decided that I was in charge of keeping an eye on her to make sure she was okay with what had transpired. If I saw that she was acting strangely, I'd need to get in contact with my brothers, so we could figure out the best course of action to keep the woman quiet.

In essence, I couldn't leave her side for a few days until I was sure she wasn't going to freak out and until the body of the man I'd just helped kill was well-hidden and on its way to being unrecognizable. The fact that she had so many secrets that she was willing to forego narcotics to ease the pain of a broken hand told me there was a lot more to her than I'd realized.

Preacher was going to have a field day with this information.

"Why are you taking me back to Jenn's?"

I looked over at Paula and grinned before I explained, "I'm not. I'm Jenn's next-door neighbor, and I'm taking you to my house."

"I thought we agreed I was going home."

"No, I believe you told me to take you home. I didn't ever agree to that."

"I can drive myself," Paula said with a long sigh. "I'm tired and hurting, Hook. As hot as you are, I am not up for you to attack the pink fortress right now."

"What?" I sputtered.

"The pants off dance off. Riding the bony express. Slaying the vadragon."

I was laughing so hard that I almost missed my driveway, but Paula wasn't nearly finished.

"Squishing the gibbly bits. Taking old one-eye to the optometrist. Polishing the porpoise."

"Stop," I gasped as I pulled into my garage. "Shit. Oh shit."

"I can go all night. But then again, I bet you can too."

"Fuck me," I hissed as I took the keys out of the ignition. "I've never heard a few of those."

"I've got hundreds. It's a skill. Or a curse."

"Definitely a skill."

"You still didn't explain why we're at your house. Give me the keys, and I'll head home." Paula put her good hand out for the keys, and I ignored her as I got out of the truck. I walked around to the passenger side and opened the door for her before I reached up and took her good hand and helped her down.

"I'm keeping you here, little one, at least for tonight. Nothing nefarious, I just want to make sure you're okay."

"I'm fine. I saw a doctor and got a cast. I'll even let you be the first person to sign it if you'll just give me the keys so I can go home and crawl into bed."

"You can crawl into my bed. I promise to be a perfect gentleman. I'm not going to offer to sleep on the couch, but I will promise that I won't touch you. I'm fucking tired, I've still got chores to do, and I have to be up early in the morning, so I'd like to get to bed too."

"I don't have the strength to argue with you. I will say that if you're sleeping in the same bed as me, I can't guarantee

I won't use you as a pillow. That's fair warning, and it doesn't necessarily mean I want you naked. It's more of me just using you for your body because you're there."

"I'll try to control myself then," I assured her. "You're really hard on the ego."

"I'm not trying to be. I'm sure the angle of the dangle is all well and good, but I'm in too much pain to care right now."

I sputtered again at her description but managed to hold in my laughter until I'd shown her into my bedroom. I watched as she kicked off her sandals and shimmied out of her pants before she flipped the covers back and crawled up into my bed. I moved closer to the edge of the bed to say goodnight and realized that she was already fast asleep. I propped her cast up on a pillow and headed outside to care for my animals. I was hours late with their evening routine, and I'd be hearing about it.

PAULA

The sun streaming in through the crack in the curtain was shining directly on my face, and I winced when I opened my eyes before I closed them tightly again. I was so hot that I could barely breathe with Hook snuggled up tight against my back, but it was just so comforting. It had been ages since I'd been held this way, and I'd missed it.

It felt like Hook was on top of the covers, and I thought that was chivalrous but unnecessary. We were both adults and could control ourselves. Couldn't we? Every time I'd looked at him last night, my entire body was flooded with heat. The man's body inspired pure lust. I wanted to trace every single one of his tattoos with my tongue. He had full sleeves with barely an inch of unmarked skin showing from his second knuckle all the way up to the edge of his t-shirt sleeve. I could only imagine what those beautiful muscles I'd felt under his shirt looked like covered in ink.

I felt him nuzzle my hair and wondered if he was awake too.

"Hook?" I whispered, not wanting to wake him if he wasn't already up. I was hoping he'd at least let me turn over so we could talk in the light of day if he wasn't asleep.

He didn't answer, but the arm he had thrown over my side got tighter as he snuggled up even closer. I hated to ruin such a good cuddle, but I really needed to go to the bathroom and then find my purse for some more Tylenol. I could feel my heartbeat in my hand and knew it had to be horribly swollen by now.

I felt Hook shift again and nuzzle my hair right before a loud grumble sounded from deep in his chest.

"Good morning to you, too, handsome," I whispered as I turned over underneath his arm. I opened my eyes just in time to see a huge set of teeth in front of my face right before a rough tongue licked me from my chin to my hairline. Once the tongue had passed over my face, I opened my eyes wide and tensed as a *tiger* tilted its head down and nuzzled his cheek against mine.

I stayed perfectly still but closed my eyes tightly,

going over every single moment of last night's trip to the emergency room to see Frankie and the ride to Hook's house before I fell into bed and went right to sleep.

I hadn't eaten or had anything to drink, so I knew he hadn't drugged me. I guess he could have given me a shot of something after I'd fallen asleep.

I didn't have that cotton-headed feeling you got after you'd had narcotics, though. If anything, I felt more well-rested than I had in months. So why in the world was I hallucinating about being in bed with a tiger? I laid there with my eyes closed as I assessed the situation.

I was warm in a comfortable bed. I felt like I had my wits about me and was aware of the sound of the fan on the ceiling above me and the sunshine coming in through the window. When I opened one eye, the tiger was still there, and it looked perfectly normal.

Okay, nothing about this was normal, but the tiger wasn't pink with purple stripes or anything like that.

If this was a drug-induced hallucination, it was a damned realistic one.

"Tonya!" I heard Hook hiss from just a few feet away. "Tonya, get your ass down! I told you to let her sleep, dammit. You're gonna scare the fuck out of her if she wakes up."

I tried to say something, but no words would come out for a second. I was finally able to squeak out, "Hook?"

"Oh shit. Paula, it's okay," Hook started to explain.

"I am currently wrapped in the arms of a jungle animal, Hook. I can't find a motherfucking bit of this that's remotely okay."

"Tonya, goddammit, get your ass down," Hook growled as he started tugging the big cat away from me. She did not want to leave her new chew toy, so she wrapped her huge paw tighter around my body and pulled me closer. "That's it! I'm getting the newspaper!"

"You're getting the newspaper?" I screeched. "What's that gonna do? Is she going to read to me? Are you serious right now?"

I heard a sharp smacking sound and the big cat jumped in a smooth motion to the floor beside the bed. I could hear them moving away from the bedroom as Hook cussed and the cat grumbled back. I took a second to gather my wits and made a quick plan of action.

First, go pee. Second, get dressed and get the hell out of Jumanji. Third, call Frankie and have her go ahead and call me in a few prescriptions because at this point, I needed a sedative besides a painkiller.

I jumped out of bed and picked my pants, socks, and shoes up off the floor before I dashed into the bathroom and slammed the door behind me. I was shaking so badly that it was almost impossible to lock the door, but I finally managed before I waddled over to the toilet and sat down to pee.

I let my head fall forward and took a few deep breaths while I relieved myself. One-handed, I pulled on my pants, socks, and shoes while I was seated. Once I'd finished, I stood up just as something caught my eye. Across the bathroom inside the walk-in shower was a yellow snake as big around as my thigh, and he was slithering *up* the wall as he tried to get out.

After the tiger wake-up call a few minutes ago, the snake was just too much for me to handle.

I let out an ear-piercing scream and darted toward the bathroom door, forgetting that my pants and underwear were still at my knees. My legs got tangled up, and I tried to catch myself before I hit the tile. At the last second, I remembered the damn cast on my hand. Rather than put my hand out, I tucked it against my body and twisted around to protect it before I hit the floor. My body bounced, and I *heard* my head thump when it hit the tile just as everything went black.

HOOK

"You didn't tell her you live with a fucking tiger?" Brea swore at me as I lifted Paula up off the bathroom floor and gently carried her back to the bed. Once I had her pants pulled up and buttoned, I checked her cast to make sure she hadn't re-injured her hand in the fall. Once I was sure her arm was okay, I put my hands on her head and felt around through her hair. Close to the back, I found a large bump where her head had hit the tile. "I can't fucking believe you, Hook."

I picked up the first aid kit Brea had grabbed out of the bathroom for me and finally found the smelling salts before I glanced over at my friend and explained, "She handled Tonya okay. I think she freaked out when she saw

Nana in the shower."

"Why is Nana in the shower? Jesus, Hook. *Why is Nana in the shower?*"

"So she wouldn't crawl into bed and scare the shit out of my guest!" I snapped as I opened the little vial and held it near Paula's nose. Paula came awake with a jolt and caught me with an impressive left hook that knocked me backwards. I fell on my ass just as she jumped up and stood on the bed with her arms up, ready to box. "Paula!"

"What the fuck is going on right now?" Paula screeched as she looked from me to Brea like a cornered animal.

"Girl." Brea choked out through her laughter. "Oh shit. I'm sorry. I'm Hook's friend, Brea. I know it's fucked up. I got drunk and passed out on Boss's couch one night and woke up the next morning with a skunk sitting on my chest. I feel ya."

"There's a snake in there that could fucking *eat me*!"

"That's Nana," I started to explain, but when Paula slowly turned her head and stared at me, I realized the true meaning of 'serial killer stare' for the first time. This tiny woman was downright terrifying when she was pissed. As weird as that was, I thought it was sexy. "Little one, calm down, and let me talk to you."

"Fuck." Paula swayed slightly when she put her uninjured hand up and touched the knot on the back of her head.

"Come here," I said softly as I got up off the floor. I held my hand out toward her, and she sighed and put her hand in mine. I helped her to the edge of the bed and then put my hands on her hips and lifted her down to stand in front of me. "I'm sorry I fucked up your morning, sweetheart."

I glanced over at Brea and saw her staring at me and Paula with wide eyes. She mouthed the words 'what the fuck', and I glared at her. She put her hand over her mouth and had the decency to walk out of the bedroom before she laughed at me.

"I feel like you're trying to kill me, but you just really suck at it. If that's what you're trying to do, just get it over with, Hook."

I laughed softly for a second as I held her close before I kissed the top of her hair. "I'm not trying to kill you. I was actually in the kitchen making you breakfast in bed when Tonya got away from me and woke you up."

"And the snake?"

"That's Nana. She usually has run of the house, but I put her up so she didn't scare you."

"That worked," Paula muttered drolly.

"Maybe we should go see your friend at the ER again. You've been knocked out twice in the last 24 hours. Something might be scrambled in there."

"We don't need Frankie's input, but even I'll admit that I need to be observed for at least a day. If I blackout, get confused, forgetful, or disoriented, have balance problems, or develop stomach issues, I'll need you to take me to Frankie whether I agree or not. Those are some common signs of concussion and might be an indicator of another issue."

"Okay then," I replied while my brain whirled at how easily all that information rolled off her tongue. "You forgot that I'm not supposed to let you sleep."

"That's been disproven. As long as I'm coherent before going to sleep and don't show any of the other symptoms, going to sleep shouldn't be an issue. If anything, it's the body's chance to naturally heal itself. Since a concussion is a functional injury, I should limit my physical activity and allow my brain to rest."

"Oh." Every minute I spent with this woman made me more and more confused. For a person that owned a craft business, she knew way too much about medical issues. I could make excuses for that with the ease of looking up information on the internet, but there was really no good explanation for her reasoning to avoid narcotics for her pain last night. That was still bouncing around my mind, and I had about ten theories on it. Shit. Now I was beginning to sound like Preacher. "Let's get some ice on your hand, and I'll serve you breakfast."

"At the table. Unless there's something in your living room that can kill me."

"Um . . ." I mentally catalogued the animals and reptiles that were normally in my house and nodded before I said, "You're good. Nana is still in the bathroom, and Tonya went outside to play."

"Do you usually warn the women you bring home that they could be considered prey by your pets?"

"You're the first woman I've ever brought home."

"Then who is that bitch who was laughing at me?" Paula growled. "If you tell me I'm standing in her bedroom with your arms around me, I'm going to eviscerate you."

"Eviscerate?"

"It means . . ."

"I know what the fuck it means, Paula. And 'that bitch' who was trying very hard *not* to laugh at you is my best friend Brea."

"Oh."

"Want me to introduce you?"

"No, I want to crawl in a hole and die. My hand is killing me, my face hurts, and I have one hell of a headache."

"Breakfast might help you feel better. We'll get an ice pack for your hand, your head, *and* your face, and then take a nap together."

"I'm not falling asleep in your house again, Hook. I don't think my heart could take it."

I smiled down as Paula leaned back and looked up into my face. Her eyes were swollen and discolored from the punch she took yesterday, but somehow she was still too beautiful for words.

I'd need to get a handle on that. I was here to watch her so I could cover my brother's backs, not drag her to bed and have my way with her.

Maybe I could do both at the same time.

HOOK

"How are things going with Paula?" Boss asked when we met between our properties. He knelt down on one knee, and Tonya walked right into his arms before she stood on her back legs and 'hugged' him with her paws around his neck. "Y'all having your afternoon walk?"

"Yeah, she's been cooped up in the pen all day because we had an issue with Paula this morning."

"An issue?"

"Well, she didn't know about Tonya, considering I just met her yesterday. Anyway, Tonya's a cuddler, and Paula woke up this morning being spooned by a giant feline with bad breath."

"Oh shit!"

"Then she went into the bathroom and saw Nana and fell and bumped her head. Knocked herself clean out. When she came to, she was, well, understandably upset."

"You think?"

"And Brea was there laughing at her. That didn't help anything."

"It's not like Brea to be mean," Boss said with a straight face before both of us started laughing. Once we'd caught our breath, he said, "Did Paula forgive her?"

"Once she figured out that Brea and I weren't a couple, she got over her snit, and the two of them had a good laugh about how stupid I was not to warn someone about a full-grown tiger and eight-foot python."

"When does Nana go home?"

"Her owner picked her up about an hour ago, which is good because I'm keeping Paula at my place tonight."

"You worried about her frame of mind?"

"About yesterday? No. I took her to see a friend of hers that's a doctor and that made me worry about an entire list of shit, but not a damn bit of it has to do with her keeping yesterday under wraps."

"What do you mean?"

"How much do you know about Paula?"

"She's Jenn's friend." Boss shrugged. "Jenn's a damn good woman, and I'd guess she'd surround herself with the same."

"Will you go fishing for me?"

"What for?"

"See what Jenn knows about Paula's past, her family, that sort of thing."

"What are we worried about here?"

"If you broke your hand, would you let the doc give you pain meds?"

"You ever broken a bone? That shit hurts. Of course I would."

"Paula refused pain meds last night because she didn't know me well enough to be off her game. She was adamant that she wouldn't take any narcotics unless she was around someone she could trust with any secrets the drugs might make her spill."

"What kind of fucking secrets can a 40-year-old woman from Tenillo, Texas be hiding?"

"And that's why I want you to go fishing and find out what Jenn knows about her friend."

"Consider it done."

"Keep this between us."

"Like you had to say it."

"She fell asleep about half an hour ago," Brea said softly before she tipped up her glass and drank the rest of her tea. She got up and rinsed her glass in the sink before putting it in the dishwasher. She turned around and stared at me for a minute. "Explain to me why she can't go to her friend's house to rest up."

"I want her here with me."

"You took one look at her and knew she was the one? You just can't let her go because you want her so bad? I highly doubt you got there in 24 hours. I get that you're a caretaker, Hook - God knows you take care of me and Sis just by being you, but what's the new fascination for housing the damsel-in-distress?"

"She needed some help last night and then she knocked herself out on my floor. What am I supposed to do? Wake her up with smelling salts, pat her on the ass, and send her home?"

Brea squinted her eyes. "She knows something, and you've got to keep her close." I didn't acknowledge that with an answer, but she knew me well enough to understand my silence. "You and the guys did something, and she saw it?"

Brea and I stared at each other for a few minutes and then she nodded once before she picked her purse up off the bar and walked toward the door. Before she got there, she stopped and stood with her back to me like she was contemplating something. Finally, she turned around and walked back over to me, stopping when there were just a few inches between us.

"If what she knows is something that can change the lives of my family, *the men* in my family, I can take care of it. I know you, and I know Boss. Neither of you have the stomach for hurting a woman."

"What are you saying, Brea?"

"I am a woman and hurting one doesn't make my stomach hurt at all if it's necessary. For my guys, my family? It's necessary."

"Thanks, babe."

"I don't need your thanks for my loyalty. . You call if

you need me. I like Paula, and I think she and I can be friends. I want to meet Boss's woman soon too. She sounds like a pistol. However, if either of them do something that puts my family in danger, the part of me that wants to be their friend will disappear."

"Gotcha."

"Take care of yourself, Hook."

"If I can't do that, I know you'll take care of me."

"Damn right."

I watched Brea walk out the door and stood there thanking my lucky stars I had a friend who was as true and loyal as Brea. I was just about to head to the kitchen to start dinner when I heard Paula behind me.

"She loves you, but not like I first thought."

"She's my friend."

"She's your family," Paula corrected.

"How much did you hear?"

"Enough to know that I should be very careful in how I treat you, or I'll have a formidable enemy," Paula explained as she walked closer to me. "Everyone needs someone they can depend on like that. I'm glad you have her."

"Do you have someone like that?"

Paula turned her head and looked out the front window. We watched Brea turn left when she got to the road, and the two of us were quiet for a few minutes before Paula answered, "I had family like that. Now I have Frankie."

She sounded so lonely that I couldn't resist pulling her close. It seemed that no matter how many times I reminded myself that she was just a woman I was trying to keep an eye on to make sure she wasn't going to spill our secrets, I just wanted her close to *me*. She fit in my arms perfectly.

Paula wrapped her arms around my waist and laid her head on my chest. It took a little bit, but she finally relaxed into me, and I felt an emotion come over me I didn't recognize. Some primal part of me wanted this woman to stay right there in that spot forever. I felt like I should tell her that she'd be safe, that I'd take care of her.

Shit.

Before I could analyze what I was feeling, Paula spoke as if she'd read my mind, "Thank you for taking care of me, Hook."

"Anytime, little one. Anytime."

Paula and I stood there together for quite a while until she pulled back far enough to look into my face. She smiled as she studied me and then asked, "Am I still a hostage?"

"Need to keep an eye on you after that last bump on the head, babe."

"When you take a hostage, is it customary for you to drive her to her house for a change of clothes, or will I have to make do and steal some of yours?"

"You're the size of my thumb. If you want clothes, I'll drive you to your house so you can pack a bag and then we'll come back, and I'll feed you dinner."

"I'm a little afraid to be here now," Paula admitted. "I braved the bathroom because I really had to pee and realized that the snake escaped."

"Nana's owner came to pick her up," I explained with a short laugh. "I've had her for three months while a friend of mine had work done on his house. She couldn't be there while it was going on because it wasn't safe for her. The work is finished, and he took her home, but if you want to go visit, they don't live far from here."

"I'm good. Thanks, though."

"Are there any other animals that freak you out?"

"Other than the tiger?"

"Tonya."

"Yeah. Her. Is there a pride of lions that visit in the evenings or an alligator living in the guest bathroom?"

"Nope. Tonya's the only one who lives in the house with me."

"And where exactly is Ms. Tonya now?"

"She's in her enclosure until dinner time when I'll bring her back in for the night. You can get to know her then."

"Has she ever tried to eat any of your houseguests?"

"I told you, you're the first woman I've had overnight at my house."

"I guess I'll be getting to know your pet over dinner

then?"

"I guess you will. Let's run over and grab your things. On the way home, we'll stop and get Tonya a toy for you to give her this evening. She's pretty easily bribed."

"I like your house," I told Paula as I followed her inside. She moved over to a panel on the wall and punched in the code to disable the alarm.

"I love my house, but I've been thinking of getting something out in the country so I can build myself a she-shed for my work. It seems like my little business is slowly taking over my house. I either need more space, or I need to get a workshop."

"What exactly do you do?"

"I started out making jewelry because I was bored. Frankie wore a pair of earrings I'd made for her to work, and one of the nurses got my information because she wanted a pair. I made a few pairs for her, then she gave my name to a friend and so on. I'd made myself a t-shirt that said something funny on it, and a woman at the grocery store asked where I bought it. I told her I made it, and she put in an order for twelve of them for her mom group. Next thing I knew, I was getting custom orders, so I started a website, and here I am. I set up at a lot of craft fairs and bazaars, but that's mostly just to get me out of the house. I have enough traffic and business coming from my website, but I like getting out sometimes."

I looked around the house and recognized that she

wasn't living large, but she did have quality furniture and electronics. I wondered just how much a pair of earrings went for these days. I honestly didn't think that making jewelry and t-shirts would afford her this house, but I could be wrong. She had to have some outside source of income.

"Have you ever been married?" I blurted out, wondering if she got the house in the divorce or walked away with a nice settlement.

"I got divorced right before I moved to Tenillo to be closer to Frankie. What about you?"

"I was engaged before I went to prison, but she wasn't the type to wait 18 to 24 years for a ceremony. So, no, I've never been married."

"Why were you in prison?"

I turned my head and stared at her for a second. "That's not really something you just ask a person, little one. With you hanging around me and Jenn, you'll be around lots of people who have served time. I'd rather you not start off on the wrong foot by asking other people that."

"Lesson learned," Paula said softly as she held my eyes with hers.

"I went to prison for three counts of manslaughter. I beat three men to death in an alley after I found them trying to rape a waitress who'd walked out behind the diner where she worked to have a smoke."

"Shit."

"You want me to drop you at Frankie's house now

instead of coming home with me for dinner?"

"What? No. I just want to know what kind of people were on the jury that could convict a man for doing a public service. A bunch of fucking assholes, apparently." I burst out laughing and Paula smiled at me before she asked, "This might be another faux pas, but why are you called Hook? What's your real name?"

"I was a professional boxer before I went to prison. I'd slowly worked my way up the ranks and was six months from my first televised match when all of that happened. I beat the men to death with my bare hands and I guess that's frowned upon even if they're trying to hurt a woman. According to the prosecutor, I should have stopped when they lost consciousness."

"Where's the fun in that?"

"What the fuck?" I blurted out through more laughter. "Bloodthirsty little thing, aren't you?"

Paula just lifted one shoulder and rolled her eyes. "So it's Hook like a right hook, then?"

"Exactly."

"What's your real name?"

"Dwight York."

"Your name is Dwight?" Paula's nose wrinkled up like she'd smelled something bad as she studied me from head to toe. She looked back up at my face and shook her head slowly. "You are *not* a Dwight."

"My driver's license disagrees with you. What's a

Dwight supposed to be like then?"

"Dwight is an eight-year old who picks his nose while he's playing goalie for his private school's soccer team. That boy either grows up to marry the girl who beat him in the spelling bee, or he becomes the assistant to the regional manager at a paper company. He does not grow up to look like you."

"I didn't go to private school, and I never played soccer. I've also never worked at a paper company or been the regional manager of anything."

"You missed your calling then, and it was the assistant to the regional manager. You really need to watch some Netflix, man. You completely missed the joke there. I'm going to pack a bag. Make yourself comfortable. I'll only be a minute."

I watched Paula walk down the hall and go into what I assumed was the master. I wandered around her living room, kitchen, and dining room while she was gone. There were a few paintings and other things on the walls, but I found it odd that there were only two photographs displayed. Both of them were of Paula and Frankie and both of them were recent. I recognized their surroundings and knew exactly where the pictures had been taken in Tenillo.

How strange was it that she didn't have *any* pictures of family or other friends? Even I had pictures of my parents around, and they'd been dead for years.

"Question."

I turned around and realized Paula had come back and was standing behind me next to the couch.

71

"What's up?"

"Are we going to see people or just hang out at your house?"

"I'm not planning on taking you out for a steak dinner. We'll do that on our third date."

Paula tilted her head and stared at me for a second before she raised one eyebrow. "Is that your roundabout way of asking me out?"

I sighed because I knew it had been, and I shouldn't even be thinking of going there. This woman was the good friend of Boss's old lady, she was obviously hiding something huge, and she knew some secrets that could put me right back behind bars. I shouldn't trust her. Hell, I didn't trust her. But for some fucking reason I was dying to get my mouth on her.

I didn't even realize I'd moved until I had her in my arms, and my mouth was on hers. She was as still as a statue for a good 10 seconds and then she was *all in*. Her arms went around my neck, and she lifted up on her tiptoes as she tilted her head for a better angle. Within the next second, I had her feet off the floor, and she was up in my arms with her legs wrapped around my waist as we devoured each other. My dick was rock hard in an instant, and if the way she was wiggling on me was any indication, she was just as turned on.

It could have been two minutes or 20, I wasn't sure. I finally pulled back to catch my breath. Paula stayed still with her eyes closed as she took a few deep breaths and let them out slowly. She opened her eyes and stared into mine before she said, "I'm going to need a few more minutes, Hook."

I started to move my mouth closer to her again,

thinking she wanted more, but she shook her head and smiled at me.

"You just turned a corner and took us down a road I was secretly hoping for from the beginning. Since that's the case, I'm going to need to take a few minutes in the shower and pack some different things in my bag."

"Why?"

"When a girl knows she's about to get laid, she's gotta have some time to prepare, big guy, especially when it's been a good long while since that's happened to her."

"A while?"

"A good *long* while."

"Same," I admitted. "Are you on the pill?"

"I've got a scar that's proof I don't need the pill."

"Can I lick it?"

"You can lick anything you want, as much as you want."

"Can I lick it before I fuck you ungloved and come inside you until you're making a mess all over my bed, then we can roll over to the dry spot and make it wet too?"

Paula didn't say anything because her mouth was hanging open in shock. For a second, I thought I might have gone too far, but there was a fire in her eyes that told me she was down.

"I take that as a yes," I told her as I let her slowly slide down my body until her feet were on the floor. "Take your time, little one. I think it's going to be well worth the wait."

Paula didn't say another word, she just walked back toward her bedroom. I felt a slow smile come over my face at the thought of making her speechless. I wanted to do exactly what I'd said and then some.

The fact that this had started out as a babysitting mission to make sure she wasn't going to fuck us over be damned. I'd wanted her since the minute I pulled her into my arms in Jenn's kitchen. I didn't know what it was or why I'd instantly felt that way about her, but it made me feel damn good to know she felt it too.

6

PAULA

Once I shut the bedroom door behind me, I leaned against it and tipped my head back while I closed my eyes and assessed what had just happened in my living room. That gorgeous man had kissed me. He'd *picked me up* and held me off the ground while he'd kissed me like I had *never* been kissed before.

And the things he said. Oh hell. I was so worked up right now that the urge to throw open the bedroom door and call him in here was almost overwhelming. Just a little quickie to take the edge off sounded like the best idea I'd had in awhile.

No. I needed to shower and shave before anything even close to that happened. I also needed to rethink the bag I'd packed. It had some of my comfiest pajamas, a pair of plain white panties, and a t-shirt I'd owned for at least 10 years. I'd packed it thinking there was no way the man would even look twice at me, so I might as well be comfortable while I was at his house.

You know what? The only thing I was changing in that bag was the panties because I didn't want a soul to see me in those. The rest was me, dammit, and I wasn't going to change that for any man. This really couldn't go anywhere anyway. That's why I'd avoided entanglements since I came to Tenillo. I couldn't explain my family or where I'd come from, and that was not the way to start a relationship.

I was going to walk into this with my eyes wide open and have a whole bunch of naked fun time with the hot man in my living room. Once that started to wane, I'd just have to talk to him and explain it was fun while it lasted for that short time, but we needed to just stay friends because we had Jenn and Boss in common.

Yeah. I could do that. I'd just make sure he didn't get attached. But who was going to stop me?

I thought about that as I hurried through my shower. Once I was shaved, exfoliated, and lotioned, I got dressed in a comfy pair of leggings and one of my favorite t-shirts. I brushed out my hair and decided to let it air dry, then started to put on makeup and just shook my head at my reflection.

My eyes were a little less swollen, but the bruises around them were getting darker by the hour. No amount of makeup was going to cover that shit. I did have a trick that I'd learned while I was married to help get rid of the bruises. I dug through my medicine chest to find what I'd need. Once I'd added all that to my bag, I took a deep breath and walked back out to find him, ready to go now.

Hook wasn't in the dining room where I'd left him, so I went into the living room. He wasn't there, so I walked out onto the porch and found him stacking boxes to bring inside.

"Hey! You don't have to bring in my mail!"

"You're not going to carry this shit! What's in here anyway? Did someone send you rocks?"

I held the door open for him. "Those are just craft supplies I ordered. I have another few boxes coming in sometime today with custom shipping envelopes and stickers. I wonder when that will be here."

"This is all the guy delivered while you were in your room. He seemed shocked to see me and asked if you were okay."

"Oh, that was Roger," I explained as I led Hook into my craft room.

"Are you two friends?"

"No. He's my UPS guy."

"You order enough stuff online that you and the delivery guy know each other by name?"

"Is that weird?"

"I'm not even sure I have a mailbox at my house, babe. I damn sure don't know the delivery man."

"I like shopping online. Sue me," I told him with a grin. "I think I keep the company Roger works for in business."

"Doing your part for the economy."

"Exactly. I'm so glad you see it my way."

"Right now, I'd agree to damn near anything because all I can think about is getting you back to my house and fucking you so hard you see stars."

"Why do we have to wait to get to your house?"

"Huh?"

I walked closer to Hook and reached out to pull on the

hem of his t-shirt. I tugged, and he moved closer to me as he stared down into my eyes. I lifted the hem and put my other hand underneath. I heard him hiss when my cold fingers touched his warm skin.

"You heard me, big guy."

"Fuck yeah." Hook's voice was deeper than I'd ever hear it as he yanked his shirt over his head and tossed it to the side. When confronted with all that hard muscle covered with just a light sprinkling of dark brown hair, I felt my eyes go wide. I was eye level with his nipple, and without even thinking, I stuck my tongue out and licked it like a lollipop. I heard him growl, so I swayed a little to the left and licked the other one before I looked up into his brown eyes that were so dark they were almost black. "Mind your cast."

"Huh?" I asked, confused until he yanked my shirt up and started tugging it over my head. Once it was untangled from my cast, my shirt joined his somewhere on the floor of my craft room. He had my leggings and panties down over my hips within seconds and then he squatted down on the floor to help me step out of them. I had just pulled my leg out and kicked the pants to the side when Hook hit his knees and pushed me back into the wall. He reached out and hooked his hand behind my knee and yanked it up over his shoulder. Before I could even get my balance and figure out what was going on, he planted his face right in my pussy.

He found my clit instantly and started flicking his tongue back and forth as he put one hand up between my legs to hold my sex apart for better access. He pulled my clit between his lips and hummed. I couldn't help but scream. I grabbed his hair with my good hand to pull him away because it was just too much too soon, but he hummed again.

Instead of pulling him away, I yanked on his hair to hold him closer to me.

I locked the knee holding me up just in time because Hook used his free hand to lift my other knee and push it up so that it almost touched the wall beside me, spreading me out in front of him. He used his fingers to push up inside me in rhythm with his tongue flicking back and forth, and I gasped when his eyes opened and he stared up into mine.

"Fuck, Hook," I whispered as he watched my face. I could feel my orgasm building already, and I prayed he'd keep doing everything just *exactly* like he was right this second. "Don't stop. Just like that."

He hummed against my clit again and tugged on it with his lips as his fingers stilled inside me. I felt them move again and then they curled and hit a spot inside that I'd had no idea existed. He hummed again as he stroked that spot deep inside, and I threw my head back and screamed through the most intense, mind-blowing orgasm I'd ever experienced. He kept moving his fingers and kept at my clit with his mouth, drawing out my orgasm. It seemed like just as it would start to wane, he'd move his fingers again and there was another surge, making it last even longer.

I was hoarse and gasping for breath when he stopped suddenly and stood up in front of me. I was in the air and spinning around before I could even get my eyes open. I gasped when my back touched the top of the cold desk beside us. Hook pushed my legs out to the side and spread me wide right before he surged into me, filling me up and stretching me to fit him before he pulled out almost all the way and did it again.

I still had a fist full of his hair and pulled his head toward me as he fucked me so hard that the desk bumped into the wall over and over again. Finally, his lips touched mine in a fiery kiss. He never lost his rhythm as he fucked me, and I felt myself tightening around him, ready to come again. Already.

The man was a machine, and his thick cock filled me up just perfectly every time he pushed into me. I heard him grunt and then he pulled his mouth away from mine and whispered, "Let go. Do it again. I want to feel it."

As if my body was obeying his command, the next orgasm hit, and my body clutched at his. The sound that came out of my body was like nothing I'd ever heard before. It was a primal yell from deep in my chest. I heard Hook grunt and then he let out a loud roar as he slammed into me one final time. I felt my pussy clutching at him as his cock twitched inside of me.

Spent, he collapsed over my body and touched his forehead to mine as we tried to catch our breath.

"Sorry, little one," Hook whispered as he stared deep into my eyes.

"For what?"

"It's been a long time for me. That was too quick. I'll make it up to you next time, I promise."

"Big guy, you've got absolutely *nothing* to apologize for. That was . . ."

"I can do better. I just need a few minutes," he assured me.

"Hook, if you do any better, it will probably fucking kill me."

Hook grinned and kissed me, this time soft and sweet. It took some effort, but I lifted my legs up and wrapped them around his waist, pulling his body as close to mine as I could get it as I reveled in the afterglow of the most intense orgasms I'd ever had in my life.

I could still feel him inside me, but I wasn't stretched and full now. He was spent and like he said, we'd be doing this again soon.

The thought of another round like this one was almost too much to comprehend. I shivered and my pussy convulsed with one last aftershock. Hook pulled his mouth away from mine and hissed. He pulled his hips back, and I unhooked my feet so he could move away, but he had other ideas. He pushed back into me and grunted as his head fell down beside mine.

I liked that what I'd done affected him, so I intentionally squeezed him again. He pulled out and slowly pushed into me again, and I realized that his cock wasn't softening anymore. It was well on its way to rock hard and ready for round two.

"Oh my God," I whispered as Hook lifted his head and grinned. "Already?"

Hook started fucking me again, this time slowly pulling out and pushing in hard so that he bumped my clit with every stroke. "I told you I'd make it up to you, little one. It's been a while for me. I won't recover this quickly every time, but I'm damn sure not gonna waste this one."

The desk was hitting the wall again, and I heard more of my shit fall onto the floor, but I didn't even care. I'd have to buy a new desk and completely redecorate my office after this. There was no way in hell I'd ever be able to sit here and work without counting all the orgasms I'd had. At the rate we were going today, I'd never get any work done.

While we'd been inside the toy store to find my gift for Tonya, Hook had answered a phone call from his office manager about a litter of puppies that had been dropped off at the end of his driveway. From the quick description he'd given me as we drove to his house, the puppies were in bad shape, and he wasn't sure he'd be able to save any of them.

He'd opened the front door of his house, given me a quick kiss on the lips, and slapped me on the ass right before he rushed toward the building that held his office.

Now I was alone in his house, and I was going to take my time looking around. I'd been here last night and this morning, but almost all of my time had been spent in his bedroom. I knew that when he came back, that's probably where we'd end up, but I wanted to spend a few minutes getting to know this man.

Hook's house gave 'open concept floor plan' a whole new meaning. The master bedroom just to the left of the front door had sliding wooden doors that met at the corner. When they were pushed open, the bedroom was visible from almost every part of the house.

I realized that the room to my right had the same

doors, and so did one up ahead in the far corner. The doors to those rooms were wide open, and from here, I could see everything inside them.

The one next to me was a home gym full of exercise equipment. He had one of those stationary bicycles I'd seen on television. I walked closer and pushed a few buttons just to see if it was as cool as the ads made it look. I wondered if he'd let me use it now and then. Maybe I would get the fitness bug if it felt like I was biking around the countryside or something.

I laughed at the thought because I knew that was never going to happen.

When I walked out of the gym, I stopped next to the pool table and studied it for a minute. It was beautiful and well taken care of, but I could also see that it got quite a bit of use. On the wall next to it was a rack for cues and such, and I noticed that none of them matched. If I had to guess, I would think that was because the people who played here with Hook had their own cues in the rack, which meant they played here often.

That was food for thought. The man belonged to the motorcycle club, I knew that, but from what Jenn had told me, only three of them lived here permanently. The other men had only come back to town after their mentor, an adorable old man called Pop, was shot and almost died. He was in a rehab facility now, recovering from his gunshot and the open heart surgery that followed, and the men in Hook's club were hanging out to make sure he was okay and help figure out who'd shot him.

I'd met Pop once before when I went to visit him with

Jenn. After five minutes, I wanted to help find the person who'd shot him and deal with them in a way that would ensure they were never able to do such a thing again. He was just that damn cool.

I walked past the pool table into the living room. There was a huge L-shaped couch that had all the bells and whistles: cup holders, reclining seats, adjustable headrests, the works. It was made of black leather and smelled divine.

As a matter of fact, the entire house smelled nice. I'd noticed before that Hook's room smelled like citrus, but in this room, I could smell leather. I glanced around and noticed a small wax melt lamp plugged in and knew that was most likely the source of the smell.

On the other side of the expansive room was another couch, this one made of the same leather but smaller. It was facing the opposite direction as if Hook had separated the room without a wall. The side I was standing on was for pool and television. The other side of the room was like a library with built-in bookshelves and a comfy sitting area.

I walked around the couch to the bookshelves and found that every one of the books was well taken care of but obviously had been read. There were biographies of serial killers, true crime books, what looked like every John Grisham and Tom Clancy novel in print, and quite a few others from popular authors. I was pleasantly surprised to see that he had the entire set of Sue Grafton's alphabet series and three shelves of Patricia Cornwell. J. K. Rowling's collection was there too. That made me smile.

Look at the big guy, enjoying some female authors. Ten points to Gryffindor!

I turned back around to look at the other big room. There was a huge wooden desk with a giant leather chair behind it, some filing cabinets, and a buffet that had another wax warmer and a few framed photos on display.

I walked closer and saw Hook as a child in the photos. I picked up one and studied it. He looked like he was about 10, and there was a smiling woman standing beside him with her arm around his shoulders. She was wearing a waitress uniform complete with the apron, and Hook was proudly holding a trophy of some sort.

The woman was thin, and even at that age, Hook was a stocky boy. They didn't look much alike, but I did see a slight resemblance. She had wispy blonde hair while his hair was thick and dark. Their smiles were the same, though. There was no doubt they were related.

I put that photo down and picked up the one next to it. Hook was standing next to the woman again, but this time, there was a man on his other side. All three of them were smiling, and again, Hook was holding a trophy.

I realized I was smiling right along with them, happy that Hook had a childhood like that. I thought back to all the pictures of me and my parents together that had been scattered around the house where I grew up. I wondered if any of them were still there or if they'd been hidden away like me.

I needed to ask my brothers if they could send me some. I only had one picture of me and my parents, and that was from my wedding. I was damn sure not going to display *that* in my house. In all honesty, I'd almost set it on fire with the rest of the shit that reminded me of Tony, but I was glad now that I hadn't. It might be the only picture I ever had of them.

I shook off my thoughts and put the picture down. I didn't see anything else of interest so I walked out to the kitchen. It was set apart from the rest of the space by an L-shaped bar surrounded by tall beautiful leather stools with padded leather seats.

There was an island in the kitchen with a butcher block top that looked like the perfect place to prep for a meal. There was a six-burner gas stove with a gorgeous farm sink next to it and a stainless steel double oven to top it all off. It was a great set-up. I wanted to go home and remodel my kitchen to look just like his.

The appliances were all top-of-the-line, and I noticed that every surface was spotless. I looked back over the house and realized the entire place was spotless. There wasn't a speck of dust anywhere. Instead of shoes piled beside the couch, there was a basket filled with crocheted afghans. There were no magazines on the coffee table, only a stack of coasters.

Hook's house was a showroom, but it still felt lived in and comfortable. The man had to have secrets somewhere, but I wasn't going to find them here. There had to be a man cave full of beer cans that smelled like sweaty gym socks somewhere else on the property. For some reason, maybe it was the biker persona, I would never have guessed the man lived in a house like this.

The man was a fucking unicorn.

I noticed there was a hallway tucked away beyond the

wall of bookshelves, so I crossed through the kitchen and went to explore. Maybe I'd find that junk room full of old Penthouse magazines after all.

The doors here also slid to the side rather than swinging in or out. I paused in front of the first one and slid it open an inch or two so I could peek inside. He'd told me that his tiger was the only pet that lived here, but after the snake incident this morning, I was leery.

The first door I opened was the laundry room and pantry, and I didn't see any reptiles or animals with big teeth in there.

I moved on to the next door and did the same thing, sliding the door a few inches to the side to peek. When nothing jumped out at me, I opened the door all the way and stood there stunned.

The room had a tree trunk in the corner that had branches hanging into the middle of the room. It was incredibly realistic, complete with lines in the 'bark' on the trunk and clusters of bright green leaves that looked like they'd be individually placed. One wall was covered in a wooden platform that had cubby holes and flat areas that were covered in different materials. There were big stuffed animals all over the place.

I was standing in the middle of a tiger's bedroom. It was like all the things I'd seen over the years that cat owners had for their pets, but on a much larger scale. I reached up and tugged on one of the low hanging branches and was surprised that it barely moved at all. I pulled a little harder, and it still didn't move.

He'd built his pet tiger a tree she could climb and given her different places to lay around and snuggle her stuffed animals.

Holy shit. That great big muscled biker was a big fluffy marshmallow who loved his pet so much that he'd built her an entire room of her own. It was sweet enough to make me want to cry a little bit.

Shit. Between the orgasms and the cat tree, I might just fall head over heels for this guy if I didn't watch myself.

The next room was a bathroom, and I was happy to see that the shower was empty. It was a normal bathroom and spotless like the rest of the house. My exploring over, I walked back to the front door and picked up my overnight bag, ready to unpack and get comfortable. I'd noticed a huge bathtub in Hook's bathroom earlier and thought it might be a good idea to have a relaxing soak.

After our sexcapades at my house where he fucked me twice on my desk and again in the shower, I was feeling a little sore down south. I needed some Tylenol not only for my hand and the bump on my head, but also for the muscles I hadn't used in *years*. If he was up for another round later, I wanted to be prepared.

Sore or not, the things that man could do with his hands, mouth, and cock would be well worth the pain.

7

HOOK

I was walking back to the house with Tonya when my phone rang. Preacher's name came across the screen, and I answered with, "Preacher man, are you calling to save my soul?"

"We're years past that, brother. I'm calling to check on the woman."

"She has a name, you know."

"Yeah, her name's liability."

I didn't want to analyze why it irritated me so badly that Preacher seemed to be gunning for her. He was just trying to protect us all from prison.

"It's Paula, and she's fine. There was a hiccup this morning, but it's all good now."

"A hiccup?"

"Tonya woke her up by jumping in bed for a cuddle and then when she went to the bathroom, she saw Nana camped out in the shower. She damn near lost her fucking mind."

"I'm going to have to side with her on this, man. Nana scares the fuck out of me, and if I didn't know Tonya, she would too."

"Well, she calmed down, and it's all good. She hasn't even mentioned what went on yesterday."

"Boss said her hand was broken, and she refused pain meds as long as she was with you."

I shook my head, not even surprised that the men were talking about her. I knew it was suspicious, and I'd been trying to ignore it all day long.

"I don't know why, but I understand why that would make you curious."

"Curious? George is fucking curious. I'm more than curious. I started looking for her footprint, and the girl's got nothing. No debt, no history, nothing."

"So it's suspicious that she's good with money? Does she rent her place or own it?"

"Owns it outright. Paid in full. Never even applied for a loan, as a matter of fact. Same with her vehicle."

"Where did her money come from?"

"Do you think I'd be asking you shit if I knew? No. I have no fucking idea, and I can't find any trace of her before she moved to Tenillo seven years ago, man. She was born a full-grown woman with a hefty bank account. There's no record of her *anywhere* before then."

"She knows the doctor at the hospital. Frankie something. Romero, I think. They were childhood friends, and that's why she moved to Tenillo. And she speaks another language. I couldn't tell what it was, I just knew that they weren't speaking English. Spanish maybe?"

"That gives me something to start with, at least. I talked to her yesterday, and she doesn't have an accent. I couldn't hear Texan or anything else."

"I noticed that too."

"The doctor called her pickle or pickle-ah or something. See what you can find about that. Maybe the doctor's name will lead you there."

"Maybe. I'm running something for Boss right now, but I'll get back to the mystery woman in a bit. What's your take on her?"

"I think she's good, man."

"And you're already fucking her. We could use that, though. If you get in . . ."

"I'm not fucking her for information, Preach. We're grown adults who walked into it with eyes open, and what we want to know about her has nothing to do with it."

"And he's defensive. Fuck," Preacher grumbled, mostly to himself, but I heard him loud and clear.

"Again, I'll say I think she's alright. There's some things I'm curious about, but they have nothing to do with yesterday."

"What are they?"

"I'll figure them out. You just worry about what you worry about, and leave me to my own shit."

"Defensive."

"You got anything else to say?"

"Keep your eyes open no matter what your dick tells you. That's all I've got to say."

"Well, that says enough then," I barked right before I hung up on my friend. I'd stopped not far from the porch, and Tonya was laying in the grass a few feet away watching me. She could tell I was pissed, and that always perked her up. I squatted down beside her and rubbed her belly for a second as I gathered my thoughts.

I needed to keep in mind that I didn't know shit about Paula. Maybe she'd open up, but maybe she wouldn't. Either way, I was going to need to keep my head on straight. I'd ask her some questions, and maybe I'd get some answers that would satisfy my curiosity and Preacher's too.

But the fact that she didn't exist more than seven years ago was a red flag waving in the breeze. No one just appeared in small town Texas like that unless there was one helluva story somewhere.

I stood up and waited on Tonya to get on her feet before I walked up the porch steps into my house. I heard the music right before the smell hit me, and I didn't know what shocked me more. Five Finger Death Punch was blaring out of my speakers, and my house smelled like fresh bread.

"Be good, girl," I warned Tonya as we walked through the house toward the kitchen. "You already scared the fuck out of her once today."

"Hey, big guy. I hope you're hungry and don't mind that I made myself at home in your kitchen." Paula came around the corner and stopped dead in her tracks when she saw Tonya. "The pizza has about 15 minutes left in the oven, so you'll have to pull it out and set it aside before you start cleaning up my blood off the floor."

"Okay, here's the scoop on Tonya. Yes, she's a big cat and could kill either one of us. At some point, she could snap and tear either of us limb from limb. However, she's been with me for two years now, and I've never once had her even play too rough with me. She's got some health issues that make her much smaller than other tigers of her kind. She was born in captivity and bottle fed from day one, but she's still a wild animal."

"Hence why I think she's going to kill me."

"When she came to us, she was so sick that I almost lost her five times that first week. We came about this close," I held my fingers apart just a little bit and then continued, "to having to amputate her front left paw because of infection. For three weeks, she had to be fed through a tube in her nose because her mouth was so infected. Through all of that, she never once tried to bite any of us who were working on her."

"Why did she almost lose her paw, and why was her mouth infected?"

"Her mother was in a circus, and not one of the big ones that you see advertised. They took Tonya when she was just a few days old and started bottle feeding her human infant formula. As soon as her canines came in, they pulled them and declawed her while they were at it. She was weak from her diet. The man that did all that to her had no fucking idea what he was doing, and it nearly killed her."

"Did someone cut his fingers off and yank out his

fucking teeth?" Paula asked in a deadly calm voice as she looked from Tonya back to me. "Because if they didn't, that's what I want for Christmas."

I ran my hand over my face and bit my tongue to keep from telling Paula just exactly what me and Boss had done to the man but decided that if we were still seeing each other next Christmas, I'd tell her about that day. Considering her outlook on vengeance, it wasn't hard to imagine us together for a while.

"Because of her circumstances, Tonya doesn't have the defenses that her breed usually has by instinct. She's as big as she's probably ever going to get and because she's never been socialized, she can't go to a sanctuary or zoo. That's why she's still here as my pet and always will be. I've got a permit to keep her."

"I just want to hug her, the poor baby."

"How about if I let you feed her instead?"

"Like with a bottle?"

"No. She eats meat. I get it delivered every three days from a butcher in town, and he changes things up for her. I think the meat du jour is a chicken and ground beef blend."

"Do you grill it or what?"

"She doesn't eat cooked meat, little one. Her species doesn't have thumbs, so they never learned to work the stove." Paula glared at me, and I couldn't help but smile.

"That is so gross."

"She probably thinks salads are gross."

"Your sarcasm is gross."

"You're so fucking cute."

"Fuck off."

She looked so pissed that I couldn't help but laugh as I pulled her into my arms.

"Let me get her mat set up, and I'll get everything ready for you to feed her, okay?"

"Okay." Paula squeezed me around the waist and tilted her head back so she could look at me. "I snooped around your house. If you've got any weird fetishes or collections, I couldn't find them. Your hiding spots must be epic."

"I keep my toenail clippings in a Ziploc in the bottom drawer of my dresser." Paula's lip curled up, and I felt her whole body tense. I let her go and walked toward the pantry, slapping her ass before I got too far away. "I'm joking. They're in a jar in the freezer."

"I enjoyed dinner."

Paula smiled at me from her spot at the end of the couch where she was curled up reading a book. We were both relaxed after the big meal she'd made, and Tonya was snuggled up on the other couch with her new stuffed hippo. I realized the time was right for the girls to get to know each other.

Or for me to fish for answers.

"Tell me about yourself, little one. What should I know about Paula Clewley?"

"I like long walks on the beach, and when I'm queen, I'll end world hunger."

"Really? I'm trying to be that guy who's interested, and you blow smoke?"

"There's not much to tell, so it's easier to resort to sarcasm, I guess."

"If we're getting married on Friday, shouldn't I at least know *some* things about you?"

Paula laughed, remembering my proposal in Jenn's kitchen. "You know things about me. You know Jenn, and you met Frankie. They're my friends. You've been to my house and snooped around while I was packing a bag. What more is there to know?"

"You moved here after your divorce? Where did you live when you were a kid?"

"We had a house in Florida. Where did you live when you were a kid?"

"Houston. Tell me about your parents."

I watched something flicker in Paula's eyes before she forced a smile. "Dad was king of the castle, and until I was about 13, treated me like one of the boys. Then he sent me off to boarding school. Mom was oblivious to everything. She was raised to believe that her husband was in charge, and she never crossed him."

"What did your dad do for a living? I assume your

mom didn't work." They had enough money to send their daughter away to private school. That might explain how she had the funds to buy her house and car flat out. It was something, at least. "Brothers and sisters?"

"My brothers were quite a bit older than me, but we got along fine. By the time I left for school, they were both off at college."

"Are your parents still alive?"

"Yeah."

I waited a few beats hoping that she'd expand on that but got nothing. "Do you talk to them?"

"No."

"Why?"

"Mutual agreement." I could tell that Paula wasn't about to give me anything else, and that just raised even more red flags. "Do you have brothers and sisters? You mentioned your parents were both gone. Did that happen while you were in prison?"

"My mom died when I was 12, and my stepfather raised me after that. He died when I was in prison. He'd been to visit me a few days earlier so at least I got to see him one last time."

"Was it an accident or illness?"

"My mother was murdered. My stepfather died of a heart attack in his sleep."

"Murdered?"

"She walked out the back door of the diner where she worked to have a break and was attacked by three men who raped and beat her. She went into a coma and never woke up."

"Holy shit. Did your lawyer happen to mention that horrible event in your defense?"

"Yes. That's probably why I got manslaughter instead of second-degree murder. Have you ever been in trouble with the law?"

"Close, but not quite. What about your birth father? You only mentioned your stepfather."

"He took off when I was a baby, and my mom never heard from him again."

"Fucker," Paula said under her breath as she turned her head and watched Tonya. "What are we doing here, Hook?"

"I told you, I'm trying to get to know you."

"That's not what I mean. Us. Me and you. What are we doing?"

"What kind of question is that?"

"You're watching me because I bumped my head? And now we're sleeping together? That's what kind of question."

"I thought we were getting married on Friday," I joked. Paula stared at me, waiting for me to answer her questions. It wasn't a lie when I said, "I like spending time with you, clothes on or off, little one."

"I'm not that fucking little," Paula grumped. "I'm 5'2"."

"I am a foot taller than you. You're relatively little. You want me to quit calling you that?" Paula thought about it for a second, and the look on her face told me she'd just realized she'd painted herself into a corner. She liked my nickname for her but wasn't willing to admit it. "I'm probably not gonna stop."

"I could kick your ass, you know."

"Wanna wrestle?"

"Maybe."

"Bring it."

Paula smiled and glanced over at Tonya. "If I whip your ass, is she going to eat me?"

"Why don't you crawl down here to my end of the couch and let me eat you?"

"I'll do it, but only because you need practice. You're not all that."

"I'm not? Hmm. I guess I should keep working at it then."

Paula moved her legs around so they were in front of her and then bent them at the knees as she slumped down further into the couch. Her head was resting on the armrest and she stared at me, waiting for me to make my move.

I didn't make her wait long at all.

8

PAULA

"Yes, I spent the weekend with him," I explained to Frankie as I pulled up in front of my house. "And no, I'm not sure if we're dating or what."

"How are you not sure? Was it a weekend fling?"

"Maybe? I'm not sure! I think he was babysitting me to make sure I wasn't going to spill any secrets, but then it turned into more. I left him in bed this morning and walked next door to Jenn's house to get my car. I think I was avoiding some uncomfortable morning-after thing so I could stay in this post-orgasmic happy bubble."

"So he knew what he was doing? That's good."

"He could teach classes. I can barely walk, and I wince every time I sit down."

"Look at you. He didn't just knock the dust off, he rearranged the furniture."

As I walked across the grass, I saw through the glass of my front porch that the front door of my house was wide open. I turned around with a gasp and rushed back to my car.

"What's wrong?" Frankie asked frantically.

"Someone broke into my house," I explained as I jumped back into my car, wincing when my ass hit the seat.

Frankie was still on speaker, and when my phone reconnected to Bluetooth, her voice boomed out. "What do you see around you? Are there any cars you don't recognize?"

"Blue sedan parked three doors down. Never seen it before. White two-door car parked at the end by the stop sign has Oklahoma plates," I told her as I sped down the street toward the convenience store a few blocks away. "I'm finding people."

"Get to a crowd. Have you talked to your brothers? Shit, would they even tell you?"

"I haven't broken the agreement," I told her as I pulled up in front of the convenience store and shut my car off. I grabbed the phone and my purse and jumped out of the car and ran inside with Frankie still on speaker. "I'm calling the cops, but I'll stay here until they go inside."

"I'm on my way." I could tell by Frankie's breathing that she was running out to her car.

"You stay out of this, Frankie. I'm going to hang up and call the cops."

"You're at the store by your house? Just like the plan?"

"I am," I answered. Before I could say anything else, Frankie hung up on me. I knew she was on her way, and in a sense, that made me feel a little bit better. Certain people who wanted me dead wouldn't do anything if Frankie was nearby. Her family was just as powerful as the one that wanted me dead, if not more so.

I called 911 and explained who I was, what was going on, and my current location. The dispatcher spoke to me in a calm voice and got all of my information as she assured me she was sending units to my home and to me. She told me to call back if I needed her and let me go.

I glanced around the small store and took in my surroundings. There were cameras in all four corners of the room, and I could see myself on the CCTV screens behind the counter. When Frankie and I had searched for safe spots, this one was at the top of our list. The owners of the store were serious about their security. That might not help me this minute, but it would damn sure give the cops something to go on if I ended up dead.

My phone rang, and I answered without even paying attention to who was calling.

"You left without even a goodbye kiss?" Hook asked in a teasing voice.

"Hey." I tried to sound normal, but I knew I'd failed by his reaction.

"What's wrong?" There wasn't any reason to lie, so I told him where I was and why. "Good call, little one. Whoever broke in could still be inside. I'll call Boss and get him on it. I'm on my way to you now."

"Oh, you don't have . . ."

"Shut it. I'm on my way. Stay right where you are."

Hook hung up, and I stood there watching the street. I could see my house from here, and there wasn't any movement around it. If there was someone inside when I got home, they had probably gone out the back when I took off. A look around the convenience store made me feel safe. There was a woman with a little boy on the candy aisle, two teenagers over by the chips, and an elderly man getting a cup of coffee. I doubted any of them were assassins sent to kill me, although I could be completely wrong.

I turned back toward the street and watched my house. In another minute, two police cars pulled up in front of it. Three officers got out, and as two of them approached my house, the third stood beside his patrol car and stared down the street at the store as if he knew I was there. I looked closer and realized the cop who was looking for me was Boss. Hook must have called him after all.

Frankie drove up and pulled into a spot right at the front before she hurried into the store. She threw her arms around me and pulled me close. I had to fight back tears as I hugged her back.

"It's probably just a regular everyday break-in. I'll go home and all of my electronics and underwear will be gone or something."

"I've seen your underwear, missy. Nobody's stealing that. Speaking of, if you're going to keep banging the tattooed veterinarian, we need to go to the mall and find you something more appealing than Hanes Her Way." As if he'd heard her talking about him, Hook pulled into the parking lot and stopped his bike right behind my car. Frankie and I watched him swing his leg over and walk toward us, and I heard her breathing get just as fast as mine. "Good Lord, that man is fucking hot."

"Isn't he?" I whispered.

"He's like sex on two legs. I wonder if he has a brother."

"I've seen the men he calls his brothers, and I must say, any one of them could be on the front of a romance novel, all tattooed and muscular. They've got the bad boy vibe down, that's for sure."

"I really want to be bad," Frankie whispered as we watched Hook come into the store. "I want to be a very bad girl."

I stifled my laughter and looked up at Hook's face as he got closer to us. Without a word, he pulled me into his chest. "Are you okay, little one?"

"I'm fine. I didn't go inside, I just got back into my car and came here."

"Good call," Hook said as his phone rang. He pulled it out of his back pocket and put it up to his ear. I was close enough that I could hear Boss's voice when he told him that my house was trashed. Hook said, "We'll head that way now."

"My house is trashed?"

"I guess so. He needs you to go down there and see what's missing."

"Damn." Frankie swore and shook her head, but I could see that she looked just as relieved as I felt. "Just a regular break-in."

"What else would it be?" Hook asked as he pushed me back so he could look at my face before he stared at Frankie.

"I guess I watch too much television. I had visions of some weirdo waiting to pounce after I was inside," I admitted, although I left out the part where the weirdo was sent specifically to kill me.

"I have to get back to work," Frankie told us as she stepped back, her eyes on Hook. She knew she'd slipped up by admitting she was glad it wasn't anything more than your average home robbery, and she wanted to get out of the line of fire before he started asking more questions. "If you need me, just call. You can stay at my place until we get yours cleaned up."

"Okay, I'll . . ."

"She'll stay at my house," Hook told her as he pulled me close again. "I'll have her call you."

"Uh, sure. That sounds good too. It was good to see you again, Hook."

"Same, Frankie."

"Stai al sicuro e chiamami."

"Certo amico mio," I murmured as Frankie walked away. I asked Hook, "Should we go down there now?"

"What language was that?"

"We studied it in school together," I lied, not answering his question at all. Frankie and I almost always spoke to each other in the language we'd grown up speaking. It seemed to bring us comfort since we both missed our families. However, we were usually careful to make sure no one heard us. That would bring about too many questions.

Obviously. "Can we go now?"

"Sure. I'll meet you down there," Hook said carefully as he let me go. We walked out to the parking lot, and he opened my door for me. I heard him chuckle as I stepped onto the running board and climbed in. "You're so tiny that you could make a house out of this rig."

"I like it," I told him. "It makes me taller than most people on the road."

"That's the *only* time you're taller," Hook mumbled as he leaned in and gave me a quick kiss. "See you down there, little one."

"Okay."

I waited until Hook had pulled away and then backed out of my parking space and headed back to my house. Once I was there, Hook opened my door and held his hand out to help me get down, then held it in his as we walked toward the porch. Boss stood there watching us as we got closer to him.

"I've got a tech on his way to do fingerprints, so I'll need both of you to make sure you don't touch anything."

"Is it bad?"

Boss stared at me for a second and then tilted his head before he answered, "It's confusing."

"How so?" Hook asked.

"I can't see that anything's missing, but Paula might know."

"Someone just trashed my house?"

"It looks like they ransacked your place looking for something."

"I'll have to check the cameras."

"The cameras are on the floor. They yanked them out of the wall. But if you can look at the video, we'll be able to see whoever was in your house before they did that."

"I'll have to log on with my laptop . . ." My voice trailed off as I stepped into my living room. "Holy shit."

My house looked like a bomb had gone off. Everything had been pulled out of the cabinet under the television and was strewn all over the floor. I walked farther into the house and saw that the drawers in the kitchen had all been dumped onto the floor and tossed to the side. One of them was broken and laying in pieces among the utensils and things it had held.

In my bedroom, all the drawers from my jewelry box had been dumped on the bed, but the room was fine otherwise. My bathroom and the guest bathroom were untouched, but the closet in the guest bedroom had been torn apart and rummaged through.

I turned and went into my craft room where the other two officers were standing and I gasped. My supplies were scattered everywhere. There were beads and bottles of paint all over the floor. The desk where Hook and I had sex was cleared off. Everything we'd picked up after our tryst was back on the floor. The drawers had been pulled out and dumped. All the pens and tidbits that had been in the middle drawer were in a pile on the seat of my desk chair.

"Can you tell if anything is missing?" Boss asked as the other two officers left the room.

"The tubs are gone," Hook told him at first glance. "There were plastic totes stacked in that corner over there. What was in them, Paula?"

"I stored my inventory I took to craft fairs in them," I replied quietly, thinking of all the hours I'd spent building my stock only to have it all stolen. "All of the custom work I was doing was sorted out in a flat tote over here, and it's gone too."

"They took your jewelry?" Boss asked, confused.

"There were three totes full of t-shirts and other stuff, too, but yeah. All the jewelry I'd made is gone." I could hear the tears in my voice, and I realized Hook could too when he pulled me into his side and rested his arm across my shoulders. I put my hand up over my mouth to hold in a sob before I whispered, "All that work for nothing."

"Your computer equipment seems to be fine as does everything else in here. Strange that none of it was taken."

"All of her electronics are still in the living room too," Hook added. "They broke in and took the jewelry she'd made but not any of the expensive shit they can pawn?"

"That does not make sense at all," Boss mused as he looked around. He turned to me and asked, "Were you making fucking gold jewelry with rare gems in here or what?"

"Costume jewelry. There were a few silver items, but no gold."

"Why the fuck would someone break in and leave the things worth something but take the cheap stuff?"

"I can't fill my orders now," I muttered as I thought about all I'd lost. "I mean, I can, but I'll have to work day and night to catch up. I'll have to start today. I've got stuff to mail out by Friday at the latest, and I've got that bazaar at the ladies club this weekend. Oh shit. I'm never going to recover. It's going to take me days to get this place cleaned up."

"I'll help," Hook assured me as he pulled me into his arms. "We'll get it done."

"You've got to work. You can't just stay here and help me clean my house."

"Let's take your stuff to my house so you can get to work, babe. We'll gather all this up and move it there for a while. You can sort it out once we're at my place. I've got plenty of room."

"No, I need to . . ."

"This doesn't make any sense, Paula, and I agree with Hook. Take your things to his house until we get this sorted out. There's no way these fuckers came over here to steal beads and t-shirts. Something else is going on, and you don't need to be here alone until we figure it out."

"But I . . ."

"Get her packed up. I'll see if Jenn's busy. If she's not, she can meet y'all at your house and help your girl. I'm headed back to the office to talk to Wrecker."

I felt Hook reach over and use one finger to push my

jaw up as I watched Boss walk out of my office. "Did he just tell me what I'm going to do?"

"He does that, hence the name."

As I turned around to assess the damage again, I muttered, "I'm going to end up helping Jenn bury him out in a field somewhere. I can see it now."

"What?" Hook sputtered before he laughed out loud.

"What? I said I liked his hair."

"Did you get everything sorted out?" Brea asked as I walked back into Hook's office where we'd set up tables for the girls to help me sort the beads and things from the wreckage of my craft room.

Hook and I had used the dustpan to pick up everything on the floor and dump it into one of the empty totes I had stored in the guest bedroom, and now the girls were sorting out the beads and other small items into the plastic divided containers that had been emptied.

"I did. Hook made fun of me when he found out my UPS guy and I were friends, but this just shows him! I called my guy Roger, and he's going to bring my packages out here for me until I get back home. Boss is going to pick up my mail before he comes home every day, and I can grab it from Jenn's house in the evenings."

"And I thought Boss and I moved quickly," Jenn mused. "You're moving in three days after meeting."

"I'm not moving in with him. Your boyfriend informed me I was staying here until they figure out who broke into my house. Does he boss you around like that?"

"Oh yeah," Jenn whispered, but I knew she wasn't talking about regular everyday stuff by the blush on her cheeks and the faraway look in her eyes.

"That is so repulsive," Brea muttered as she, too, watched Jenn's face. She shuddered, and I laughed at her.

Jenn was still off in lalaland thinking of sexy time with her man when I asked Brea, "You've never thought of dating any of Hook's friends?"

"I was married for ages. My husband passed away a couple of years ago. So, no. I've never dated any of the guys."

"Are there any of them that *don't* repulse you?"

I watched Brea's cheeks heat up and knew she was lying when she said, "Nope. Not a single one of them interests me in the least."

Jenn snapped out of it to help me tease Brea. "Which one is it that you think naughty stuff about?"

"I don't."

"Liar," I teased. "You want to do the no pants dance with one of them. Don't try to lie."

"They don't see me like that. I'm just their old friend, Brea."

"The no pants dance? Really? Where do you come up with this stuff?" Jenn asked with a laugh.

"It's a gift."

"Where's Hook now?" Brea asked, trying to change the subject.

"He and Boss went off with the guys somewhere. They were awfully vague, so I assume it has something to do with whatever they're doing with Sin and his guys," Jenn told us. "He said they're all going to come back here, and we'll have pizza for dinner."

"I should put some more beer in the fridge then," I said as I stood up and walked into the kitchen.

"Look at you. Third day of the relationship, and you're already the perfect hostess for Hook's get-togethers," Brea took the chance to tease me back.

"It's not a relationship," I argued as I walked into the pantry. "We're just . . . I don't know what we are yet."

"He let you move your stuff in here, and I saw two suitcases by his bed. If it wasn't a 'something', then why are you staying here instead of at your friend Frankie's? Or at Jenn's?"

"That's a really good question," Jenn agreed.

"Because Boss said this was where I needed to go."

"And you obey his edicts because . . .?" Brea pushed.

I pretended I didn't hear her and dropped down in front of the refrigerator to make room for the case of beer I'd found in the pantry. While I was down there, I wondered exactly why I didn't put up more of a fight when Boss ordered me to stay with Hook. I also wondered exactly why Hook rolled right along with it.

Hook was a perpetual bachelor. You could see that by looking at his house. The pool table, the arcade game over in the corner, the ten-gallon water bottle by the fridge that was half full of beer bottle caps, and the neon signs promoting his favorite football teams and beers that hung on the walls all pointed to a man who was set in his ways and liked his house to be party central. Those signs did not point to a man who wanted a woman to settle down with him in this home.

I was playing house, simple as that, and I needed to watch myself. I had too much going on worrying about my family to get settled in with a man like Hook who asked way too many questions and pushed until I was almost tempted to tell him the truth about myself.

I had to be on my toes when I was around him because he seemed to spout random questions when I wasn't expecting it, like this morning when he asked me what town I grew up in while we were toweling off after our shower. Or over coffee when he said, "What do your brothers do for a living now?"

I didn't know why he was so intent on learning about my family, but I did know that I couldn't give him any details. I was Paula Clewley now, and Hook would have to be content with that. He didn't need to know the sordid details about how I became her, just that I *was* her. Paula Clewley, woman without a past. That was me.

I stood up and broke down the beer box before I folded it up and put it beside the trash can. I turned around and saw that Brea and Jenn were talking now bent over the work they were doing at the table, and I was glad their attention wasn't on me anymore. As nice as it was to have two new friends, they needed to only know about Paula Clewley, not the woman I used to be.

After all, I wanted Hook, his friends, and my new friends to stay safe. If I told them all about who I was and where I was from, I couldn't guarantee that.

And sadly, if they didn't quit pushing me for information, even inadvertently, I'd have to disappear from their lives just like I'd disappeared from my own.

9

HOOK

"Paula!" I yelled as I rushed through the front door of my house.

Paula jumped up from the desk and hurried my way as she asked, "What's wrong?"

"Jenn was attacked at her place, and they rushed her to the hospital. She lost a lot of blood."

"Oh no," Paula whispered as she picked her bag up from the table and slid her feet into the boots she kept by the door. "Take me to her."

Paula and I rushed out the door, and I got onto my bike. As I started it up, she jumped on the back and wrapped her arms around me, ready for a ride she knew was going to be fast. We got to the hospital in less than half the time it usually took and rushed inside only to find that Jenn had already been taken up to surgery.

The nurses in the emergency room were helpful and directed us to Stamp and Boss. We took the stairs instead of waiting on the elevator. When we came out of the stairwell, I could see Boss and Stamp, both dressed in scrubs, sitting next to each other in some chairs at the end of the hall. Sin, Executioner, and a few more of the Ares Infidels were there along with almost all of my brothers.

As we got closer, Paula let go of my hand and wove

115

her way through the men to get to Boss. She didn't say a word, just pushed his arm out of the way, sat down on his leg, and wrapped her arms around him in a tight hug. Her purse fell to the floor with a thump and dumped out a handful of her stuff, but she didn't even seem to hear it. She was huddled up with Boss, and his arms were tight around her as the two of them silently prayed for the friend we'd all come to love.

"Did they say anything?" I asked Preacher when I stopped beside him.

"She lost a lot of blood. We're going down in shifts to donate."

"I'll go too," I murmured as I looked around. Sin and four of his men had bandages in the crook of their arms, along with Stamp, Kitty, and Santa. When Bug, Captain, and a few more of the AIMC guys walked up, they had bandages in the ditch of their arms too.

"Our turn. Are you coming?" Chef asked as he turned to go down the hall. I glanced over at Paula who still had her arms wrapped around Boss and back at Chef before I nodded. We were standing in front of the elevators when I asked, "Has anyone called Brea?"

"I called her. She and Sis are with Pop right now. She's going to tell him that Jenn was hurt leaving out the details I gave her. They'll be up later."

"Brea's coming up here?" Chef asked as we walked into the elevator. "Haven't seen her since I've been home."

"I don't know how. That woman's all up in everyone's business just like old times," Preacher complained. "If it wasn't for that girl of hers, I'd have washed my hands of her by now. I swear she picks fights with me just so she doesn't have to argue with the fence post."

"I saw Sis at the shop when I went in the other day, but that's all. How's Brea?" The intense look on Chef's face didn't match his nonchalant tone of voice as he asked about our old friend. "Is she getting along okay since her husband passed?"

"She's at loose ends, trying to stay busy. She's doing the books for me and Pop, working at an office part-time, working at my clinic part-time, and still has the time to get under Preacher's skin."

"She dating anyone?" Preacher slowly turned his head and stared at Chef with wide eyes, and I realized I was doing the same thing. "What? Am I not supposed to ask that question?"

"When your voice breaks like a thirteen-year old asking the head cheerleader to go to the school dance, it makes a man wonder if *you've lost your fucking mind!*" Preacher ranted. "If you start dating that woman, I'll just go ahead and take you out back to put you out of your misery, brother. She'll be all up on your ass harping about shit that's none of her fucking business. *'Why are you eating that? That shit's going to kill you. Mountain Dew is going to rot your stomach, Preacher. Cheetos aren't really a dairy product, you need to eat a more balanced diet. You need a haircut. Your clothes are falling off, I need to take you shopping. You have bags under your eyes, you need to sleep more.'* Jesus, it's like being married without all the benefits in the sack."

I had to put my hand over my mouth to hide my smile.

Preacher put himself around Brea on purpose almost every single day, and I knew he did it because he enjoyed the attention when she mothered him like she did the rest of us.

"She mothers me when I see her too, man. I'm not gonna date her. I'm just one of her projects."

I stared at Chef and realized the big man didn't like that thought at all. I wasn't one to meddle, but Brea was the sister I'd never had along with being one of my closest friends. She'd been broken when her husband died, but she'd rallied. She'd healed enough that she was just looking for something to fill her days now.

If she would turn her focus to Chef instead of sparring with Preacher, maybe my friend could find the kind of happiness Paula was bringing into my life.

"She's got to be okay," Preacher said right before the doors opened. "If Jenn dies, we'll lose Boss too."

"Jenn's not gonna die, Preacher man. I have a good feeling about who her trauma surgeon might be, and that woman would give her everything to save a patient."

"Who's the surgeon?" Preacher asked.

"Paula's best friend Frankie. The one I told you about."

"Oh shit. I read up on her. Everything said she was the best around these parts and one of the top in the country."

"Let's hope that's right," Chef said in a voice so low that it was almost a whisper. "Jenn's our girl now. She's gotta be okay."

HOOK

"Hey, baby," I murmured before I kissed Paula on the top of the head when she snuggled up against me.

"Morning, sweetheart."

"You want to wake your man up with a smile for the day?"

"Are you my man?"

"You're here with me, aren't you?"

"Are you sick of me taking up half your bed?"

"I feel like for the past few weeks, we've barely been in my bed. Now that Jenn's home from the hospital, things should quiet down some. Boss is taking time off to be with her, and I hired a new tech to take care of her animals a few times a day. Now that things are calmer, I'll have you all to myself again. Besides, a little thing like you barely takes up any space at all compared to the only other female that's slept in my bed."

Paula lifted her head and looked behind her where Tonya was sprawled, still sleeping. "She's such a good guard cat."

"Shit. She'd sleep through someone robbing the house." I felt Paula wince and instantly apologized, "Sorry, little one. That hit a little too close to home."

"It's okay. Speaking of my house, don't you think it's

safe for me to go home now?"

"You want to go home."

"I didn't say I wanted to be anywhere else but here . . . however, I do *have* a home if you want me to be somewhere else."

"It's not safe, babe."

"I call bullshit. But if that's the way you want to play it, we can go with that."

"I like having you in my bed and knowing you're safe. If you're all the way across town, I don't have either of those things, do I?"

"I've lived all alone in that house for almost seven years, Hook."

"And then a month ago, someone broke in and tore the place apart for no reason."

Paula was pensive for a minute before she agreed, "You're right, but does that mean I never go back?"

"You like it here?"

"Well, obviously. I'm not a hostage."

"You want to go back?"

"I . . . well . . . no."

"Are you my woman?"

"Yes, Hook. I'm your woman."

"Then wake your man up by giving both of us a smile, little one." Paula giggled and then let her hand trail down under the covers until she had her hand wrapped around my cock. I was already hard, and the feel of her cold hand wrapping around me made me hiss out a breath. After a month, she knew just how to touch me to get me there, but since I'd woken up with her naked body beside me, it didn't take much for her to have me close to the edge. "Hop up here, babe. Let me have my breakfast."

Paula turned so that she was straddling me, and I reached up and lifted her to bring her body back so that her knees were on either side of my shoulders. Just as I felt her mouth around the head of my cock, she eased her hips back and let me taste her. I lifted my arms up and wrapped them around her legs until my hands were gripping her ass, pulling her down even lower until she was sitting on my face. I pulled her clit in between my lips and hummed just the way she liked. I heard her whimper before she ground down on my mouth and took me even deeper into hers.

My woman liked how I ate pussy, so I took every opportunity to remind her how much she enjoyed it. After just a few minutes, I finished down her throat after her entire body tensed and then relaxed with her first orgasm of the day.

I turned my head to the side and nipped at her thigh so she'd lift up a bit. She moved forward to give me breathing room and collapsed against my chest. Even though I had already finished, her hand still stroked me slowly while she rested her head on my thigh.

"You keep doing that, and you're gonna get another one, babe," I warned her.

Paula laughed softly and then started to lave my balls with her tongue. I let her play for a few minutes while I used my fingers to explore her again. We stroked each other leisurely, worshiping each other with our hands and mouths until I was hard again. Finally, I slapped her on the ass and growled, "Assume the position."

Paula giggled and swung her leg over me so I could get up. While I stood, she turned so that she was spread wide in front of me with her ass in the air and her face down as she clutched a pillow to her chest. I stood there studying her as I ran my hands over her ass and then leaned forward and notched the tip of my cock right where it wanted to be.

She let me know that she'd had enough slow and easy when she pushed back and took me inside her all the way to the root. I slapped her ass before I grabbed her hips and got to work, moving faster now as I pulled almost all the way out and slammed back into her with every stroke. I wanted to come but wanted to hear more of the sounds she was making every time I filled her.

"Hook, please," Paula begged as her hands moved to clutch the sheets by her head.

"I'm playing," I told her with a laugh.

"Stop playing, and get to work!" Paula snapped, frustrated now. She started to push up, but I didn't let her, using one hand to push her back down as I leaned forward and started fucking her in earnest. With my other hand, I reached around her and cupped her sex for a second before I softly started tapping against it in rhythm with my thrusts. Paula hissed and tried to push up again. I knew she wanted more. I tapped against her harder, and when I heard her moan, I knew I'd found the sweet spot. After just a few more strokes, she threw her head back and screamed as I felt her orgasm squeeze my cock. I worked her through it and then let myself go with a roar as I slammed into her body one last time and came inside her. As I gently pulled out of her body, I heard Paula whisper, "That was a good one. In the top three so far."

I laughed as I turned around to go start the shower. When she didn't follow close behind me like usual, I walked back into the bedroom only to find her asleep with the pillow she'd been holding clutched tight to her chest. I pulled the sheets and blanket up to cover her and then leaned down and softly kissed her on her forehead before I got in the shower and started my day.

Yeah, I thought to myself. She's definitely my woman.

"Why is she still living in your house?" Preacher asked as he leaned against the fencepost and watched me work on Tonya's pen. Every so often, I came in and changed things up, moving her tall perches around and changing out the shaded area where she napped. I had a few different swings and hammocks for her, and I rotated those in and out too. She spent 10 hours a day out here, and I hated for her to be bored.

I knew what it was like to be locked up in the same environment day in and day out, and I didn't want that for her. If she had to be held captive rather than roaming free, at least she could have new scenery on occasion. It was the least I could do.

"Why shouldn't she be? Boss couldn't find anything on the video, and the people who'd trashed Paula's house were wearing gloves. In the last month, some deliveries that inadvertently went there instead of here were stolen too. It's not safe for her to be home alone."

"How is that our problem? We don't know shit about this woman, Hook, and you're still fucking her."

"Watch yourself, Preach."

"You've fucking fallen for her. Goddammit, Hook. You were just supposed to make sure she didn't spill our shit while she had a concussion, and you ended up moving her ass into your house."

"What better way to keep an eye on her, huh?"

"I mean the eyes in your skull, Hook . . . not the one attached to the little head."

"Ain't nothing little about me, boy."

"Don't change the fucking subject. Every time I ask you if you found out any more about her, you change the subject. I want to know who she is, and you should too."

"Why the fuck does it matter? It's obvious we can trust her. It's been a month, and she hasn't told a soul what happened that day. Are you on Boss's ass to make sure Jenn keeps her shit tight?"

"Well . . ."

"I didn't fucking think so. Keep your goddamn nose out of mine and Paula's business too."

"Jenn's an open book, man. It's not all that hard to get a read on her. Your girl is the opposite. She can change the course of a conversation in a heartbeat and make you forget you even asked her a fucking question in the first place. I think she's a grifter."

"A grifter? What the fuck?"

"I suspect she's a con artist. There's no other way someone could be that good at evading questions. She was probably trained from childhood or something, but we wouldn't know because we don't know anything about her family."

"You've met her friend Frankie. What did you find out about her?"

"Not a fucking thing. I found out she's a doctor, and she's got all her shit in order, but the only person that came up when I searched her name was an 84-year-old woman in Italy who won some sort of contest at a fair there last year."

"Maybe she discovered the Fountain of Youth, and Frankie's really an elderly woman from Italy. Oh! I've got it! She's a vampire, and so is Paula. They have to change their name now and then to get Van Helsing off their trail."

"Man, fuck you. I know you and the guys laugh about my conspiracies, but how often am I wrong?"

"Disney always kills off the moms so they can brainwash children to never trust their parents?"

"Look at the facts, Hook. I'm telling you . . ."

"I was using that as an example, Preach. I am not

getting into it with you again. Paula is just Paula, and I'm okay with that. I like having her here, and I know she likes being here. If she doesn't want to tell me all her shit, that's fine."

"She's hiding shit, and with all that's going on in this town, how are we supposed to be sure that she's not involved?"

"She's a criminal mastermind now? I get that she's a smart cookie, but really?"

"There's women disappearing, fucking drugs all over the place, old men getting shot on their own property for no fucking reason. Maybe she's just a side player, but she's got something to hide, and I think it's some high-powered illegal shit. There's no other reason for her to be so fucking evasive."

"I've had that woman naked in every possible position in my house. I've spent weeks with her just a short walk away. She's never done anything to make me suspect she's hiding anything from me other than the fact that she won't share her life fucking story. She's not going to fuck us, man. Get over it." I put my hammer back in my tool bag and ran my hands down Tonya's long back as I walked past where she was sunbathing on one of her new perches I'd just installed. I leaned down and kissed her nose, and she stuck her tongue out and licked my ear before I stood up and walked away. "I'm going to go in the house and shower before I eat my girl for a midmorning snack. You go the fuck home, and do whatever it is you do there and leave me to my business."

"Blinded by pussy."

"You wish you were."

Preacher scoffed, "None good enough to blind me, brother. That's why I'll be here keeping watch over you since you're obviously lost."

Preacher didn't say goodbye, he just stomped over to his bike and roared off as usual. The man was way too high strung. We really needed to find him a woman so he could take the edge off now and again.

I used a stick to try and get the mud off my boots before I went inside, but just decided to pull them off by the back door and let the mud dry in the sun. I could get it off later.

I walked through the office and waved at Linda who was eating a cup of yogurt as she watched some documentary on her computer screen. I went through the storage room to the door that led into the house and closed it behind me before I threw the lock to make sure we weren't interrupted during the little break I had planned. Paula wasn't working in the office and I didn't see her anywhere else, so I knew she must be in the bathroom. Since she didn't call out, I knew she hadn't heard me come in.

I decided to surprise her, so I snuck down the hall and peeked around the corner into our bedroom. I heard her talking to someone, so I paused in the doorway rather than interrupt her conversation.

"I can't wait to see you, too, and I've found the perfect excuse to get away." Well, that brought me up short. She sounded excited and upbeat while she was planning to fucking lie to me. "I'll leave tomorrow morning and be there right before you fly in. We'll meet at the restaurant and spend the afternoon together. I'll come back home when your flight leaves."

I felt my spine straighten at the thought that she was making plans to meet someone behind my back. I wanted to storm into the bathroom and yank the phone out of her hand and demand answers.

Preacher was right. She was hiding something, and I was too blinded by her act to see it. Fuck.

"I've got a lock on her phone, and I put the tracker on her Expedition," Stamp explained as he stood next to me at the window in my office. I could hear Linda and Leo talking to someone, and a few seconds later, Chef appeared on my other side. "Oh, I didn't say shit to Preach, but I told Chef."

"I see that. How'd you get her phone and the tracker if you didn't talk to Preach?"

"I called Sin and one of his men helped me out," Stamp explained. "It wasn't hard at all, and that sort of freaks me out, but oh well. She'll never know we're tracking her."

"She waved at me on her way out of the driveway. Where did she tell you she was headed?" Chef asked in his deep, gravelly voice.

"Said she had to run into Dallas to shop at market to get some supplies for her jewelry shit."

"This sucks, man. I liked her."

"Shit, so did I. I felt like I'd known her forever since the first time I met her," Stamp agreed. "Sorry, Hook."

"Yeah."

"How did you hold it together last night?"

"I stayed in my office with a fake emergency. Went home for a shower this morning, and that's when I got the lie about a shopping trip."

"Are you ready to go?" Stamp asked. "I figured we'd give her half an hour to get ahead of us and then head out in my truck."

"Yeah, let me tell Linda I'm out and that she needs to keep that quiet for me. I'll meet y'all outside."

10

PAULA

"He didn't even ask to go with you?"

"No, Frankie. That's what's so weird. He was distracted because of an emergency, so I didn't even see him last night. If he came home and slept at all, he was gone before I woke up this morning. When he came home to shower, I told him I'd be gone all day, and he just shrugged. I called the office right before I called you, and his receptionist said he was in with a patient, and she'd have him call me back when he could."

"That's so odd that he'd keep you at his house to protect you and not even blink when he found out you were going on a road trip."

"I'm not looking a gift horse in the mouth right now. I'm going to have my visit and enjoy my time today and then go back home to him. It's the best of both worlds, right?"

"You have to tell him, piccola," Frankie said softly. "You can't live this lie. If he finds out some other way, he'll never trust you again."

"I can't tell him. If anyone at home finds out, they'll come after both of us."

"First of all, how's anyone at home going to find out? And second of all, I don't think they'll come after you. Your son and your brothers are your protection, piccola. They'd never want to anger them, no matter how much they want you gone. You just have to stay away until that generation dies off and then it will all be forgotten."

"As long as he is alive, I won't be safe and neither will anyone else. Well, you are, of course, but that's just because your family is so much meaner than mine."

"Aww. You say such sweet things. Back to Hook. You have to tell him. You can't go behind his back taking phone calls and running off to visit the guys. What happens if Zach wants to come to town for a few days to visit you? What will you do then?"

"I never even thought about that," I whispered, more to myself than to Frankie.

"If you won't let Hook meet your son or your brothers, is it really a serious relationship? Are you going to tell them about him?"

"I planned on telling them about him today. I thought it was better to do it in person, you know?"

"I agree with that. Go home this evening and tell Hook you lied and why. Put it all on the table. That's what I think you should do."

"I'll think about it, Frankie. I promise."

"Trust him, piccola. You trust him with your body and your heart, trust him with your secrets too. I hate to cut this short, but I've got to go."

"Me too. I'm getting close to the exit now."

"Enjoy your visit and tell them I said hello. And then

go home and tell Hook the truth."

"Bye, Frankie."

"Piu tarde amico mio."

"Later."

Frankie hung up, and my audiobook started playing again, but I didn't pay attention to the words. As usual, traffic around the airport was insane, but the restaurant my brothers loved so much was nearby. Rather than deal with the airport traffic myself and go onto the grounds to pick them up, my brothers always arranged for a car service to come to me instead. I knew that one of their assistants had reserved a table for us, most likely outdoors, so I'd dressed appropriately for the cool March weather.

Once I was seated at the restaurant, I checked flight arrivals on my phone and saw that my brothers had arrived a few minutes early and were probably already on their way. I was anxious to see them. It had been months since their last visit. It wasn't often that they flew as far south as Texas, although they tried to come see me at least a few times a year.

They couldn't just arrange for a visit - that would be flaunting their disobedience in my father's face. Instead, they waited until they had an excuse, and let me know when they could make it. I'd drop anything to see them - even the man I was growing to love, apparently.

Finally, my brothers arrived, and I stood up to greet them as they walked toward our table. I couldn't hold back my tears and held onto each of them for quite some time when they hugged me. I could tell by how tight they held me that they'd missed me too.

"Paola, what happened to your arm?" Vincent asked as he held my chair for me. Once I was seated, both of them took their chairs and leaned forward to talk to me. "You didn't tell me you were hurt."

"If I'd told you how I got hurt, you would have flown down and lost your minds. I'll just start by saying that everything was taken care of in a way that the two of you would condone."

"Everything? What exactly is everything? Who hurt you?"

I glanced over at Antonio's face and saw rage there, so I knew I had to answer carefully. "A dead man."

Vincente and Antonio nodded. Neither asked a single question about how the man died or who took care of it because they knew I wouldn't be able to tell them anyway.

"Now then, tell me who has put the smile in your voice. I've heard it for a while now but didn't ask over the phone because it would be easier for you to lie to me that way," Vincent said as he reached across the table and put his hand over mine. "Who is he?"

"He's a very good man, you two. I don't want you to worry."

"Is he strong enough to deal with that mouth of yours?" Antonio asked with a smile. "He must be a saint, this man."

"Oh, he's not a saint. He's an ex-con, belongs to a motorcycle club, makes a living as a veterinarian, and has a pet tiger."

Vincent and Antonio were clearly taken aback. They looked so much alike that it was eerie, and the matching looks of concern on their faces was creeping me out.

Antonio was the first to start with the questions when he asked, "Was he helpful when that happened to your hand?"

"He and his brothers took care of everything very thoroughly."

"He has brothers?"

"Well, Vinnie, not brothers by blood, but brothers in every other way. His motorcycle club is really a family. They do everything together, including taking care of problems like mine."

Antonio scoffed, "Not very well, if he went to prison, apparently."

"That was before he met them, when he was younger. He heard a woman scream, went to see what was going on, and found three men trying to rape her. He beat them to death with his bare hands and was convicted and served time."

"That's bullshit. He should have received a commendation," Vincente argued before he took a sip of the wine I'd ordered for him.

"That's exactly what I thought!"

"Has Frankie met him?"

"Yes, Antonio. Frankie has met him. Speaking of, I was talking to her on the way here, and she asked me to say hello."

"What does Frankie think of this man? What's his name?"

"I was wondering when one of you was going to ask that, Vincente." I smiled at both of my brothers and braced for a million more questions. "His name is Hook."

"She's not trying to hide anything, meeting whoever this is out in the open like that," Chef pointed out as we watched Paula put in an order with her server. Within a few minutes, the waitress reappeared with a glass of tea for Paula, a rocks glass full of amber liquid, and a glass of red wine. "That's a good sign."

"She hid enough by lying about where and why she was going."

"Now Hook, let's think about this for a minute," Stamp argued. "When she leaves here, she very well may go and buy beads and shit."

"It's still a lie of omission if she's meeting some man."

"Two someones, and one is having a glass of wine. Could be a man and a woman."

"It's still a lie of omission. Why didn't she say 'hey, I'm going to Dallas to meet some friends for lunch before I go shopping'?"

"Are you going to ask her about it?"

"Fuck, I don't know, Chef. I mean, this all started because I needed to keep an eye on her and make sure she could be trusted. Now I've caught her in a lie, sneaking around. How can I trust her to keep *our* secret?"

"I'm going to run to the bathroom. You guys need another drink yet?"

Chef and I shook our heads, and Stamp disappeared into the restaurant in search of the men's room. We were on a patio out front across from the restaurant where Paula was sitting. I could see her clearly, and if she'd been looking around, she might have spotted us across the street. There was a busy parking lot between us and her, and she hadn't once looked our way.

A Town Car stopped in front of the restaurant, and I watched two very well-dressed men get out and walk inside. Within seconds, they were out on the patio and Paula was wrapped up in one of the men's arms. She moved to the other man and hugged him tightly too.

"She's not kissing them, brother. I think they must be related. Long hugs like that are for family you haven't seen in a while."

"Okay, what did I miss?" Stamp asked as he put his beer down and sat down next to me.

"She's meeting with two men," Chef answered.

Stamp leaned forward, and his eyes got wide. His mouth opened in shock and he stared at Paula and the men with her.

"What?"

"Holy shit. What's Paula's last name?"

"Clewley. Why?"

"Her friend. The doctor. What's her name?"

"Frankie."

"Frankie what, Hook? Is it Romano?"

"Yeah, I think that's it. I thought it was Romero, but Romano works."

"What's going on, Stamp?" Chef asked as he stared at our brother. "You know those guys?"

"Yeah, I know them. I knew them. Shit. I knew Paula looked familiar somehow," Stamp whispered. "Holy shit."

"What the fuck is going on?" I said in a low voice. I could see he was piecing shit together in his head, but I wanted to know what exactly it was that had him so freaked out.

"Francesca Romano and Paola Moretti were the reigning queens of St. Charles Catholic School until Paula was sent off to boarding school."

"What?" I barked. Paula had mentioned going to boarding school when she was 13.

"Both of them were geniuses. Seriously. Smartest people I'd ever met, and they were best friends. They liked to compete against each other for grades and shit, but it was always dead even because their scores were perfect."

"Love this walk down mobster memory lane, brother,

but you've got to spit it out." Chef was as confused as I was, but I had a better idea of where this was going.

"The Romanos, Morettis, and my family, the Russos, were in charge, but it was a kind of a delicate agreement. There was bad blood and disagreements around every corner. A few other families took care of their own shit, but they usually kept it tight on their side of the river. Sal Moretti killed my father and sister, so I tracked him down and killed him right here in Dallas when he brought his mistress down for a wedding. Those two men are his nephews, Antonio and Vincente Moretti."

"Paula's having lunch with mobsters?" Chef whispered before he turned and stared at Paula and the men.

"We don't have to worry about your girl spilling our secrets, Hook. She was trained from birth to keep her mouth shut."

"You think Paula is that girl you mentioned? Paola?"

"No, your girl is Paula, man. Paola is dead. She died seven years ago after she was admitted to the hospital when her husband tried to kill her. Before she died, she gave the cops video evidence of what he'd done. Multiple videos. She had hidden cameras in the house and recorded him beating the shit out of her. He was under suspicion for a bunch of illegal shit and that was enough to get him into custody where they worked his ass for information. He gave up some people under pressure and ran away to Italy with his tail between his legs the second they let him go. Problem was that she not only shamed his family when she sent him to jail, but she shamed her family too. She overdosed on pills at their house when she got out of the hospital, and they didn't even give her a funeral."

"She's Paola."

"Yeah, man, she's Paola Moretti, and the people she's sneaking around to see are her own brothers."

"What the hell?" I turned my head and stared at Paula. She threw her head back and laughed at something one of the men at her table, one of her brothers, said. I could hear her laughter all the way across the street.

"Does her son know she's alive?"

"Her *son*? She's got a fucking kid?"

"He runs around with my boys. He's about 25 now, I guess."

"Holy shit. No wonder Preacher couldn't find a record of her," Chef mused.

"We need to get him off her fucking trail before he sets off some red flags and puts her in danger," Stamp told me. "If she faked her death, there's got to be a reason, and that reason is enough to have her hiding in small town Texas under a fake name. If he digs in the way we know he can, he'll set off a chain of events that might get her killed."

"Her telling our secrets isn't even on the table anymore," I told my brothers. "What I want to know is when she is going to tell her secrets to me."

"You're still pissed that she lied?" Stamp asked me.

"I guess I'm not. She had a pretty good fucking reason. When she met you, did she recognize you?"

"She looked at me funny, but that was it. She smiled and shook my hand like it was nothing. But it took me until now too. I felt like I knew her somehow, and I guess that's why."

"How did you not recognize her?" Chef asked. "And you killed her uncle? Holy shit."

"Man, we haven't seen each other since the last day of school when we were 12. That was more than 30 years ago. People change."

"Wow. Her family is in the mob."

"Mafia, Chef. The mob is a whole different ball of yarn."

I heard the front door open just as Tonya jumped up from her spot at the end of the bar and walked that way. Paula's voice rang out, and I heard a thump when her big purse hit the table by the front door.

I slowly walked around the corner and watched her greet Tonya, smiling when I saw that she was already barefoot, her shoes close to the wall where she'd kicked them off the second she got home.

"I got you lots of presents, pretty girl," Paula said softly as she let Tonya drape her paws over her shoulders for one of her hugs. "I found a place online that sells stuff to zoos, and lucky for you, they had a store down in Dallas. You're gonna love what I brought you!"

Paula fell back on the floor from Tonya's weight and

laughed when Tonya started licking her cheek and huffing at her.

"She loves you," I told Paula as I sat down on the arm of the couch and watched Paula try to get away from Tonya's tongue. When she was able to get out of the big cat's arms, Paula sat up and pulled her purse closer. She dug through it for a second and then pulled out a package of wipes and washed her face. When Paula smiled up at me from her spot on the floor, I smiled back and said, "Hi, little one. How's my woman?"

"I have had the very best day, Hook. The very best. And now it's even better because I'm home with you!" Paula said as she got to her feet.

"Come here, baby." Paula walked my way and when she got close, fell straight into my arms. I kissed her softly before I pulled her tight to my chest and held on. "I missed you, tell me about your day."

"It was awesome, Hook. Just awesome. I want to tell you everything I saw, but first will you help me bring in the stuff I bought? I got some stuff for Tonya, and we can give her a few things now, but there will be more delivered later this week for us to put in storage so we can swap stuff out. I got a bunch of supplies and a new throw for the living room and ordered some towels for your guest bathroom that will match the rug you've got in there perfectly, and I found some shirts for you that I think you'll like. They're by an up-and-coming designer, but they're t-shirts that feel like cashmere . . ."

"You were thinking of me while you were gone?"

"Of course. I think of you all day even when you're close by."

"I wish I could have gone with you."

"You know what? I'm going again soon, and I want to talk to you about that. Maybe you can come with me then."

"You're already going back? Why so soon? Did you not find what you were looking for?"

"I did. I found everything I was looking for and then some. I want to talk to you about it, but right now I want to show you all the stuff I bought and then snuggle up naked with you in bed to show you just how much I missed you."

"I've got dinner in the oven, so we've got 30 minutes for you to show me all your stuff before I feed my woman and let her tell me every detail of her day. *Then* we'll get naked, and I can show her how much I missed her."

"Oh, Hook," Paula whispered as she laid her head on my shoulder and squeezed me tight. "I'm so happy right now. There are just no words."

"Think about it and find them. You can explain why you're so happy over dinner, baby."

11

HOOK

"We set the trap inside her porch, and two of my men are in there waiting with Bug." Sin, the president of the Ares Infidels MC, explained the schematics of their setup. He and Boss were working together along with their clubs to get to the bottom of all the shit that was going on in town.

In cases where one of my club brothers from Time Served MC was too obvious because of our connection to Boss, Sin's group would step in and take over. For some reason, Boss and Sin had decided to put his men inside Paula's house along with at least one of our brothers to catch whoever kept stealing her shit.

"I like that you're trying to help solve my girl's problems, brother, but why waste the manpower on some petty burglary? What am I missing here?"

"There's been six more break-ins in the last two weeks, and you want to know what they all have in common?" Boss asked me.

"Sure."

"They all run craft businesses like Paula's but on a smaller scale. Three of them reported that their mail had been stolen the week before and then four houses and two apartments were broken into within three days. One of the women was pissed that the supplies she'd custom ordered online was one of the boxes stolen."

"What kind of custom supplies?"

Sin answered, "Address labels, business cards, shit like that."

"Paula had a delivery of those get lost in shipping or so she thought. It shows the package was left on her porch, but she never saw it. Unless the asshole who likes breaking and entering is stealing shit to give to his girlfriend, these make no fucking sense. Electronics, laptops, hell, even diamonds and gold jewelry were left at each scene, but shit they'd made disappeared along with their shipping stuff. Now, it makes no sense to me why, but that's all I've got."

"Mail goes through x-ray machines, right?" Sin asked the two of us.

"It's random. They don't x-ray every package, and the person observing the machine is probably not trained for much other than being able to discern the shape of more obvious things like guns or other weapons. Maybe bombs? I'm not sure, but I have a contact I can ask."

The three of us contemplated for a few minutes while we sipped our coffee. Sin suddenly sat forward as if he'd just had one of those light bulb moments and couldn't wait to share. "If I want to ship something out in little baggies, and I intersperse them with earrings and other little shit that you can see the outline of on an x-ray, this would be the best way to do it. Add to that if the package gets opened and the drugs are found, my name isn't on it. The name of the crafty little woman who made the shit is the one they're going to go after."

"Fuck me," Boss muttered. "And we'll never even

know for sure what goes where because all they've got to do is go to the self-serve kiosk, pay with someone's debit card, and the mail's all gone. What the fuck?"

"Sin's men catch whoever's stealing the mail, we figure out who they're working for, and torture them to see who's above them. That's my plan in a nutshell." Boss said with a chuckle. "It's been a bit since we visited the wellhouse. Last time we were there, we got quite a bit of useful information."

"But why are they stealing mail now? Why keep taking the packages once they've sent their shit out?" Sin asked.

"Unless they're getting return mail sent to those addresses."

"Fuck, Hook. You've got a point. Send off some shit, when it arrives, swap it out with something you want to go back, put 'Return to Sender' on the package, and you've just shipped out whatever the fuck you want without a chance of getting caught or even paying a dime to ship it."

"We've got the guys set up inside. As soon as they catch whoever is sent over to grab Paula's mail, we'll bring them out to your place so you can talk to them," Sin told me. "I've got to go. Lyric's got a thing, and I promised to be there."

"Okay. Thanks for your help, Sin. We'll talk soon," Boss told our friend. I stood up and shook Sin's hand before I gave him my thanks and then sat back down to talk to Boss.

"Now, tell me what you three were up to that required you to ask a favor of our new friends when what you needed was stuff that Preacher could do in his sleep."

"Tell me how Pop is doing first. I haven't seen him in a week."

"He's charmed all the nurses. The fact that Jenn keeps them in snacks, and Paula has made jewelry for every single employee there also helps, but he's getting so antsy that I'm thinking about chaining him to the bed so he'll stay put."

"Brea said she goes to see him every morning for their usual coffee and bitch session. She did mention that he's getting squirrely."

"I expect a call from them any day now to tell me he's hotwired a car and taken off for home."

"How're things going with Brea running the truck for Jenn?"

"She's on top of that shit, of course. Jenn's going nuts not being able to touch anything with both hands in casts, but I'm glad she's got Brea's there all the time. Paula keeps her spirits up too. Tell me what happened yesterday."

I gave Boss the details about our trip to Dallas. His eyes got as wide as saucers as he listened to me explain what Stamp had figured out. He finally blurted out, "Your girl's in the mafia? Fucking really?"

"I guess technically, she's not anymore, but I didn't really get details. We were gonna talk last night after dinner, but we got sidetracked. By the time we were done, we were both so fucking tired that we passed out. She was still asleep when I left the house to come meet you guys."

"Are you gonna tell her that you know?"

"I think she was going to tell me last night."

"But you got sidetracked. Did she instigate that or did you? If she did, it was because she wanted to keep your mind off of it. If you did, it's because you didn't want to give her the chance to evade the truth."

"No, it wasn't like that at all. Fuck. Even knowing she's been lying to me this whole time, I can't keep my hands off of her or get her out of my mind."

"Does she know you love her?"

"I haven't said it."

"But she knows."

"Probably. She's one of the smartest women I've ever met, brother. Eerily smart. And she pops up with odd details on shit that a regular person would never know. Like the shit with Jenn's hand. When Stamp was asking me questions about the nerves in her arm, I got a detail wrong, but Paula drew him out a map of the bones, muscles, and tendons and showed him where Jenn was going to run into problems."

"Do you think she was a nurse or that she's just got random facts in her head like Rainman?"

"Fuck, I don't know. That's not the first time she's spouted medical shit that shocked me."

"What are you going to do?"

"I'm going to give her time to figure out how to tell me. I understand now why she lied. It doesn't make it go away, but it's better than it eating at me because I don't know what's going on."

"True. Give her time. She's a good woman. She's been right beside Jenn every single day while she adjusts to living at home and being helpless. It'll all come out somehow, and you two will work it out."

"That's what I'm hoping."

"I'm going by the house to check on Jenn before I go into the office. You good here?"

"Yeah. I'm going to run a few errands and head home. Let me know if you need anything, and tell Jenn I said hey."

"Will do, brother," Boss said as he walked away from the table. I watched him go and then looked down at my coffee. After I got some work done at the office, I was going to cruise over to No Man's Land - the rough section of town - with Preacher, Stamp and Chef to see what sort of trouble we could find.

Boss wasn't happy about it, but the guys and I had been roaming around the seedier areas of the city starting shit with people just to see what sort of slime rose to the top of the normal sludge that did business in that area. So far, we'd jumped a few dealers and roughed them up before we made them watch us destroy their product. After we took all their money, we'd leave them there for whoever else to find, hoping to send a message to the motherfuckers that worked the streets that life might be dangerous in their line of work, but it got downright painful when one of us ran into them.

I had not shared any of this with Paula, and I didn't plan on it. As far as she knew, we were just hanging out together for a while before we ended up playing pool and drinking beer at my house.

Our little Robin Hood ventures had netted quite a payday for a few of the non-profits in town. Chef had already decided that whatever money we got from the dealers we ran into this evening would go to a new scholarship program for kids who wanted to play peewee football but couldn't afford the fees or equipment.

A few weeks ago, he'd insisted that he'd take care of getting the money we'd 'found' to a worthy charity. A few days later, my receptionist Linda had squealed when she opened the mail and found that an anonymous donor had given over three grand to the rescue side of the clinic. When I'd confronted Preacher and Chef, the two of them had denied knowing anything, but their laughter told me otherwise.

I decided to call Torpedo and a few of the other guys from AIMC to see if they wanted to join us while we played around this evening. There was no sense in us hogging all the fun, was there?

PAULA

"They're baaaack," Brea sang out when we heard the motorcycles roar up the drive toward the house. "Who's with him tonight?"

"I'm not sure. He just said he and the guys had a thing, and they'd be home later. I didn't realize he'd be back so quickly, or I'd have had snacks ready."

"They'd be fine eating pizza, chips, and beer," Sis, Brea's daughter, informed me seriously. "I've seen them do that. A lot."

"I know, but I don't want to eat pizza and chips. I'd like some real food, so I just cook for everyone."

"I'd make them order pizza," Sis grumbled as she looked down at the bracelet she was making. "Less dishes too."

"That is true," I conceded. "But if Stamp's with them, he always helps with the cooking and the dishes. Chef does too. I have a funny question that maybe the two of you can answer. Hook told me it's rude to ask what the guys have been to prison for and I get that, but he kind of hinted it was inappropriate to ask how they got their nicknames too. But if I ask you two instead of them, that's not nearly as bad, right?"

"Their nicknames mostly coincide with the crimes that got them sent to lockup. That's probably what Hook meant by that."

"Oh." I frowned at Brea and then looked out the window to see where the guys were. "I really want to know why Chef is called that and not Stamp. Stamp is the one that cooks, not Chef. And really, why is he called Stamp? Did he used to work for the post office?"

Brea choked on the drink she'd just tipped back and started coughing. Sis laughed as she playfully slapped her mom on the back.

Once her laughter died down and she could breathe without choking, she told me, "Chef's cooking was so bad that they sent him to prison. Stamp's arrest did have something to do with mail, just like Hook's name had something to do with boxing. That's really all I can tell you."

"What about Boss? Is it just because he's bossy? That's it, isn't it?"

"Pretty much," Brea admitted.

"What the hell are they doing out there?" I asked, more to myself than anything. "They never go back to the office; they always just come stomping right into the house after their manly adventures."

"We should go be nosy," Brea urged as she stood up and leaned toward the window for a better view of where the men had parked. "Come on."

"Okay," I told her with a laugh as I jumped up and stepped into my flip flops. "Let's do it. Sis, you coming?"

"Oh hell, why not?"

Sis and Brea followed behind me as we walked through the back door of the house into the storage room of the office. I could hear the men's raised voices, and someone, I thought it might be Preacher, yelled, "Fuck, that hurts!"

"Quit being a pussy. I've almost got it and then one of you is going to have to do this for me," I heard Hook growl.

"I'm gonna call Saint. He'll help us get the bullet out," I heard a man's voice say.

"What the fuck?" I hissed as I walked through the office.

Just before we got to the door of the clinic's surgical

room, I heard Hook say, "Stop fucking whining, Preach, or the girls are gonna hear you and come out here and start crying or some shit."

"What in *the fuck* is going on?" I yelled as I hurried into the room.

"Little one! Hey!" Hook was slack-jawed and wide-eyed as he stared at me over Preacher's body. I looked around the room, and every man in there was standing with their mouths open and their eyes just as wide as Hook's. "Don't you worry about this, babe. We'll be inside in just a bit."

"You're bleeding too!" I heard Brea exclaim. When I turned around, I saw her inspecting Chef's side where his shirt was covered in blood.

"I'm calling Saint. He's better with medical shit than any of us. He'll help us out."

"You will put your phone down, sir," I ordered. "The last thing we need is more people in this room, especially if they're going to be pissed off. Chef, sit down in that chair. Brea, get over to the sink, and let me show you how to wash your hands before we glove up. Sis, get my phone out of my purse and bring it in here. The rest of you move out of my fucking way."

"Paula, I've got this," Hook told me as Preacher groaned on the table between us.

"You've got this," I mocked under my breath. As I started scouring my hands, I turned my head and looked at him when I yelled. "You've got this, my ass. You're not wearing any fucking gloves, the table he's on had dog piss on it four hours ago, and you're standing there with a second hole in your ass that doesn't belong there . . . but *you've fucking got this*. Shut up and get out of my way, Hook. I'll will both literally and figuratively get to *your* ass in a minute."

"What do you want me to do?" Brea asked as she scrubbed her hands up to the elbow with soap.

"After you have gloves on, you can put pressure on Chef's side. Hey, you, Mr. Torpedo," I addressed the man who was standing off to the side. "Grab that package of gloves off the shelf and open the corner. Don't touch any other part of it. Preacher, get up off the table. You! I don't know who you are, but I want you to spray that table down with the disinfectant there and put down one of those blue pads. Do it right now."

Everyone stood still for too long, so I barked, "I said right *now*!"

"I've got your phone, Paula." Sis said from behind me.

"Hold it over here so it will recognize my face and open. I want you to go to my favorites and call Frankie. Put it on speaker for me, babe." Sis did what I asked. I looked at Preacher standing beside the table with his pants around his knees. I was happy to see that there wasn't much blood coming out of the small hole on the outside of his thigh. The other man, the one I didn't recognize, had finished prepping the table so I motioned for Preacher to lay back down on his side.

"Piccola," Frankie's cheerful voice came over the line when she answered.

"Hey, Franks. Are you still at work?"

"Fifteen minutes to wine. Yes, ma'am."

"I just had a flashback. Remember when those three boys in the neighborhood were 22, I think it was, and they came to us for help?"

Frankie spoke slowly as she thought through the code I was speaking and carefully asked for more information, "They wanted bread and beer?"

"Yes. Probably fancier bread than just plain white. Beer is optional. I've got green tea that will tide them over if they need it."

"I was going to Uber to my house. My lease was up and my new car doesn't come in until tomorrow. If you're busy, can you send someone my way?"

"They'll be in my truck out front."

"Oh, Piccola, I must love you so much."

"As I love you."

Frankie disconnected, and Sis pushed the button to close my screen before she backed away.

"Okay, we're just going to have to roll with things until she gets here. She's going to lose her fucking mind at the thought of doing a surgical procedure in a veterinary clinic. You," I pointed at Santa before I continued, "Do you have any new holes in your body?"

"No, ma'am."

"Will you take my truck and pick up my friend Frankie from the main doors at the ER. If you'll just park out front, she'll find you. Bring her back as quickly as you can, please."

"You're a nurse?"

"Sure." I shot Preacher a look where he was laying a few feet away. I waited on him to come back with something sarcastic as I pulled on a pair of gloves and watched Brea do the same. "Chef, lift your shirt, please. Is it through and through?"

"Yes, ma'am. It's bleeding sluggishly on both sides."

"Brea, grab two handfuls of gauze and hold pressure on that. Hook, my sweet, darling, lovable boyfriend, wash up and put on gloves. I'll need you to assist, please."

Hook washed his hands and got out what I told him to before I walked over and inspected Preacher's wound. I sighed and tiptoed to get a better view before I stepped back and looked under the table to see if it had a lift. As if she'd read my mind, Sis appeared with my step stool that I'd bought to use in the pantry and set it down at my feet.

I stepped up and assessed the wound as I talked to the man on the table in front of me. "Now Preacher, this is going to hurt. I'm going to let it hurt because, well, it's your own damn fault for getting shot in the first place. When I go digging around in there for the bullet, if you yell and scream at me, or God forbid, try to hit me, I'll have one of these large gentlemen hold you down, and I'll dig that fucking bullet out with my fingers instead of doing it the civilized way."

"I'll be good," Preacher said in a very low, calm voice. I started probing the area around the wound and realized that it wasn't nearly as bad as I'd originally thought. I could feel it just under the skin. "It didn't go deep - it just skated under the skin there, Preacher. This is not going to be a problem at all, okay?"

"Good." Preacher lifted his head and smiled and then let his head drop back and whispered, "Just fix it."

"Stamp, will you come stand here? Not that I don't trust you, Preach. Okay, that's a lie. I really don't trust you not to knock the shit out of me when I get in there." I reached over to the tray and picked up the brand new scalpel and then put my fingers on either side of the bullet under the skin. "Now, I'm going to have you take a deep breath. On the count of three, I'm going to get it out, okay?"

"Okay."

"Deep breath. One, two . . ." I pushed my fingers down on either side of the bullet and sliced over the top of it. The bullet popped out and hit the table near his hip just as I said, "Three."

"Where in the fuck did you learn to count, woman?" Preacher roared as he reared up and glared at me. Stamp reached out and grabbed Preacher by the shoulders, but I knew he wasn't going to hurt me. He just needed to bluster through the pain for a second or two.

"Oops. It's been a while for me. I'll make it good for you next time, I swear. Just give me a few minutes to recover." Preacher glared at me as the men tried to hold back their laughter. I glanced over at Hook, and he had his lips pulled in between his teeth so hard that the skin around them was completely white. "Now, I'm going to clean it and put a bandage on there for you, okay?"

Preacher actually growled before he laid back down on the table with a loud sigh. Within just a few minutes, I had his wound cleaned and packed. As Executioner and Stamp helped Preacher off the table, Hook and I cleaned the space, washed up, and regloved while Sis fitted the table with a new pad and brought me another surgical tray.

"If you need something for the pain, I've got some edibles I was saving for a special occasion. They're in the medicine chest in a bottle of women's multi-vitamins. Will you get them, Sis? Okay, Chef, it's your turn. Brea, will you stand next to him? Hook, hand me that basin, please."

Hook handed me a thin basin, and I had Chef shift up so I could put it under him to catch the blood. Chef hissed when I started irrigating the wound, and I saw Brea's hands pick up one of his and hold it against her chest as she watched me. When I glanced up again, she had her lips on Chef's knuckles and tears in her eyes. I wondered for a second if she was going to be sick but then I realized she was just very upset that the man had been injured.

"That's really all I can do for you right now. I am going to pack the wound, and I'll need you to come see me twice a day for a while to make sure everything's good, okay? Preacher, I'll need to check on you twice a day too."

Preacher grunted, and I took that as an agreement. Chef answered me with, "I can do that."

"This is really gonna fucking hurt," I warned him.

"It's all good. Do what you gotta do."

I heard movement at the doorway and looked up just in time to see Frankie appear followed by Santa.

"Aww, this brings back memories," Frankie said sarcastically as she walked up to stand next to me. "I brought some supplies because I didn't know what you had on hand. I called in antibiotics to the 24-hour pharmacy. They should be ready now if one of you wants to go pick them up. I know the pharmacist, and he won't give you any lip. Just go through the drive-thru, and tell them your name is Frankie Romano. Pay in cash, please."

"I'll go," Santa offered. "Can I take your truck, Doc?"

I tilted my head when I realized he was talking to me. He smiled and raised his eyebrows in question. "Sure."

"I'll go with him," Executioner offered. "Do you need us to get anything else at the pharmacy?"

I looked around at the shelves and took a quick inventory before I shook my head. "I don't think so. One of us will call if we find we need something."

I finished with Chef and stepped down off my stool to clean up. Brea and Sis took care of the table, and I joined Hook and Frankie at the sink.

"And what, may I ask, are you fucking doing, Paula?" Frankie hissed as we stood next to each other. "You come in here barking orders like you're at home, and they're going to know you aren't just some crafty woman that sells jewelry."

"I think that cat's out of the bag," Hook said from my other side. I glared at him, but he wasn't cowed. He leaned down to kiss the tip of my nose and smiled at me. "Thanks, Doc."

"Oh, fuck you," I snarled. "Drop your pants, and let

158

me see your ass, Hook."

"Of course, baby. I didn't realize you liked an audience."

Frankie and I turned around to look at Hook, and the asshole started swiveling his hips as he unbuttoned the top button of his jeans. I heard Chef's deep voice sing "bow chicka wow wow" before the rest of the guys chimed in. Within just a few seconds, everyone was laughing, and Hook's pants were on the floor.

"Sis, you're gonna need to close your eyes."

"Get over it, Hook. I'm watching live and in-person surgery tonight, and I don't care if I have to see your hairy ass to do it."

"My ass is not hairy!" Hook argued as he used my stool to crawl up on the table where he laid facedown. He was still in his underwear, and that was fine. We could cut around it to get to what we needed.

"Can one of you take his place handing us the things we need?" I asked the men.

"I'll help," I heard Stamp say just before Frankie gasped in shock. "Hey, Frankie. Long time, no see."

"Valentine?"

"Funny meeting you here, huh?"

It was my turn to be caught off guard. My mouth hung open for a few seconds while I stared at the man.. "Holy shit. I knew you looked familiar! Valentine Russo?"

Stamp nodded before his face broke out into a big grin. "No hard feelings about your uncle, Doc?"

"Hell no. He was a total dick."

I glanced over at Hook and saw that he wasn't quite as confused as he should be, considering I'd just realized I knew one of his friends from my past life. I decided to deal with that later when I heard a commotion out in the hallway. Most of the guys had trickled into the house or gone out into the hallway. The only people left in the room now were Sis, Stamp, Frankie, Hook, and Torpedo. And then Boss and Sin walked in with fire in their eyes.

I put my hand up, and Boss glowered. "I know you probably want to ream his ass right now, but that ass still has a bullet in it, and we really need to get it out. The other two are perfectly fine now - just don't wrestle with them or anything while you yell, okay?"

"Next time someone from either of our clubs comes to you for something, you call one of us before you start working on them. I don't care if they're bleeding out on the goddamn porch. This is bullshit!" Boss roared before he stormed out of the room. I heard him further down the hall yell, "Fucking bullshit!" just before what sounded like a trash can flew into a wall with a loud thump.

"And I'll add a polite thank you and move on," Sin said gallantly, but I could tell he was pissed by the way he glared at Torpedo and jerked his head toward the door.

"Somebody's in trouble," Sis sang under her breath, and I couldn't help but laugh.

"We're going to need to deaden this. What we really

need is an x-ray, but since he's not bleeding, I'm not really all that worried." Frankie talked to herself as she poked around the edge of Hook's wound. She'd already cut his underwear so that only one cheek was covered, and now, she was bent over him trying to figure out the best way to proceed with our limited equipment. "God. Do you remember that time your brother got shot, and we had to dig it out in your basement because the feds were watching your house?"

"I do," I whispered. "Fun times."

At this point, the cat was out of the bag. No one seemed shocked when Frankie called Stamp by his actual name, and no one even questioned how I knew both of them or that my best friend and I were reminiscing about the surgical procedures of our younger years.

"This time, I planned ahead. Hook, you're gonna feel a pinch and then a burn, okay?"

"You're giving me a shot?" Hook yelled as he tried to scramble off the table. Stamp put his hand on Hook's back and held him down as Sis moved over by his head and ran her fingers through his hair. In a quieter voice, he argued, "I don't need a shot!"

"He's covered in tattoos and has a fucking bullet in his ass, but the man's afraid of a shot. I sure can pick 'em. Awfully pretty, but not all that much going on behind the eyes, you know?"

Stamp barked out a laugh, and I heard Sis trying her hardest to hold one back.

"I don't want a shot," Hook slurred.

"I already gave you the shot, dumbass. Be still," Frankie said firmly before she reached for one of the syringes she'd laid out on the tray. She pulled a cap off of one and started deadening the area, but Hook had no idea. I didn't know for sure what she'd given him, but the big man was already relaxed and high as a kite.

12

PAULA

"When Boss got home, he was so pissed," Jenn recounted before she leaned forward and sipped from the straw I'd put in the iced coffee I'd made for her. She still had casts on both hands and would for a while. Luckily, Frankie had removed my cast a few days ago, and I already had full range of motion.

That was very fortunate, considering last night's events. I wouldn't have been any help if I was still one-handed.

"Yeah, he was pissed when he got here. Sin seemed to handle it better, although when he looked at that guy, Torpedo, he did not look calm at all."

"Do we know how they got shot?"

"We do not, and I'm just gonna say that we probably shouldn't even ask."

"Well, that doesn't make much sense. I mean, who are we going to tell?"

"I'm sure that's just their way. My family was like that, like them, the men in the club, and you never asked questions."

"You never mention your family."

"Well, you're going to hear about it, and I promise to tell you everything, but I kind of feel like I should have this conversation with Hook first, you know?"

"You have a mysterious past?"

"Sort of. Okay, yeah. But the cat's definitely out of the bag since last night. I think the guys already knew, though. They didn't seem shocked at all."

"I know they had Preacher looking into you. I overheard the guys talking."

"Which guys?"

"Preacher, Boss, and Hook. They were worried that you might have loose lips. Hook defended you, though. He said he thought you would keep quiet. He said that after watching you, you didn't seem affected by that day at all."

"He'd been watching me?"

"Well, you basically moved in, so I'm sure it wasn't hard for him to realize you weren't going to go to the FBI to snitch."

"He was watching me. Keeping me close so he could make sure I was trustworthy," I whispered as I stared down into my mug.

"Paula!" Jenn frowned. "No. That's not what it was at all."

"He only moved me in here so he could make sure I wasn't going to rat him out."

"He moved you in here because it wasn't safe to go

back to your house after what happened. And then all that shit happened with me, and you two had to take care of my menagerie. Maybe that's how it all started, but I can tell by the way he looks at you that his feelings are far deeper than that now, my friend."

"I was the one eyeballing you," Preacher called out from the couch where he'd been supposedly sleeping. He'd eaten one of my special edibles last night for the pain, and rather than take a portion of the square, he'd popped the entire thing in his mouth and promptly fell asleep on the couch. I'd actually forgotten he was there until he spoke up. "Hook didn't want me to look into you. He kept telling me that you were straight, and we didn't have anything to worry about. When I got all over him about it and said something shitty, he almost took my fucking head off defending you."

"I thought he really liked me," I said quietly, ignoring Preacher who was still talking.

"Paula, he does really like you. Boss told me that he admitted he was in love with you. He hasn't said anything?"

"He hasn't said anything like that. I was just a convenient lay while he made sure I'd keep my mouth shut."

"Bullshit," Preacher barked as he stomped into the kitchen. "He pretended that's what was going on at first, but just think about all the times we've all been together. He can't keep his hands off you - always with an arm around your shoulders or holding your hand. He kisses you so much that you've probably got the same blood type by now from swapping so much spit. He hauls ass home every single day at lunch so he can see you, he's home most every night instead of out fucking around with us, he gets pissy when we overstay our welcome and he wants alone time with you . . . the man's so fucking in love that I'm surprised he doesn't fart rainbows and piss glitter. That bullet wasn't the first thing that landed in his ass cheek. Cupid's arrow made its mark weeks ago."

"God, you're so fucking long-winded," I heard Hook say from the mouth of the hallway. I turned and stared as he scratched his naked chest and then lifted his arms up and grabbed the doorframe while he stretched and yawned. "Of course I fucking love her, Preacher. Have you looked at the woman? Have you ever sat down and had a conversation with her? Jesus. Pour me a cup of coffee. It feels like my tongue is made of sandpaper, and my brain is filled with cotton."

"Good Lord, he lost his shirt," Jenn said under her breath as she studied Hook's muscular body. "And those sweat pants should be fucking illegal."

I couldn't help myself and had to agree with her. "I know, right?"

Hook took the cup of coffee from Preacher and then leaned his hip across the bar from where we were sitting. He blew on his coffee and then took a small sip.

"Your friend gave me a shot. I don't like shots."

"My friend gave you something to knock you out so you wouldn't feel us digging a bullet out of your butt."

"Why do I still feel fucked up?"

"Because that tea I forced you to drink when you woke up at the ass crack of dawn was made with marijuana.

So was the piece of candy I gave you for your dry mouth. You're probably still high."

"You drugged me?"

"I sure did," I admitted. I heard Jenn laugh softly as Hook looked down at his coffee and then over at the coffee pot. He shrugged and took another sip.

"I have to say that weed's come a long way since I was a kid."

"Ain't that the fucking truth," Preacher chimed in. "I ate one piece of candy and in 20 minutes, I was seeing giant gummy bears digging through the trash can."

"The piece you ate is generally 10 doses, Preacher. No surprise that you were seeing shit."

"Fuck! He ate 10 doses of that stuff you gave me? I had no idea you kept that much on hand. I thought you just got some for me after I got out of the hospital."

"Eh. Takes the edge off when I'm stressed." I looked over at Jenn and smiled before I wiggled my eyebrows and said, "You get off the narcotics, and we'll have a little party. We can invite Brea."

"Do not invite Brea," Hook told me. "I mean, you can, but she probably won't join in. I'm just saying."

"Okay," I drew the word out, but Hook didn't say anything more. I guessed that was Brea's story to tell just like the guy's prison information was theirs.

"Cool Cat, let me walk you home. I think Hook and the Doc have some things to hash out."

"Call me later?" Jenn asked as she leaned over for a hug. When she was closer, she whispered next to my ear, "He may have lied, but so did you. Keep that in mind, okay?"

"Okay," I whispered before she pulled away. "I'll talk to you at the same time, same place tomorrow if I don't talk to you before then."

Since Jenn was up and around now, she walked over to have coffee with me every morning. In the afternoons, when Hook went back to work after his lunch break, I usually went over to visit with her and helped Brea bake if the food truck had a gig. I'd start dinner at Jenn's and leave it in the oven for when Boss got home before I came back to our house and started our own dinner.

Our house. Mine and Hook's house.

I'd been living here for a month and hadn't even stepped foot into my own house in weeks. It was our house now, and I really hoped it stayed that way.

Holy shit, he just said he loved me!

My gaze snapped up to Hook's, and he gave me a lazy grin. "You just realized what I said earlier, didn't you?"

"Yeah."

"I do, you know. I think I have from the start."

"You can't say that yet. I've got to talk to you about a few things first. Right now, you don't even know who I am, so you can't really be in love with me."

"I know who you are. You're my little one. You're funny and sweet. Smart and sassy. You hate shoes, your hair smells like coconuts, and your pussy tastes like sweet peaches. You make these funny little sounds while you're sleeping, and when you wake up in the morning, you stumble around like a drunk and can't even speak in full sentences for at least 10 minutes. You take forever in the shower, you wash your hands at least 50 times a day, you're the first one to volunteer when one of our friends needs something, and you hate accepting help - even if you need it. You don't like to talk about yourself, and you're a master at changing the subject. You take care of me and Tonya like you were born to do it, and you seem to enjoy doing it to boot."

"But there's more, Hook. I haven't been honest with you because I really shouldn't say anything. The people I'm afraid of are people that you should be afraid of. If they found out that I . . ."

"If they found out that I know you're really Paola Moretti and you're really supposed to be dead, they'd be pissed off. I really want to know the hows and whys, but I have to admit, I heard you on the phone arranging a secret meeting, and I was fucking pissed. I got Stamp to help me track you, and we followed you to Dallas and watched you meet those two men. Stamp recognized them and in turn, recognized you. That's how I found out who you really are. Now I want you to forgive me for being a jealous ass, and tell me why you're hiding."

"You were protecting yourself, big guy. It wasn't so much jealousy as much as it was self-preservation."

"It was 50/50, little one. Oh, and I really want to hear about your son. Tell me everything, sweetheart, and then tell me why you can't see him either."

"Oh, Hook," I whispered as tears streamed down my face. The relief was almost overwhelming that I could *finally* talk to someone about my son. "He's such a little shit, but he's my little shit. But he's really not little. He's as tall as you and hilariously sarcastic. Two months ago, he turned 25, and when he called me, I sang "Happy Birthday" like I do every year. We're going to meet in Vegas this fall, and I want you to come with me. I think he'll like you. I know he will. Anyone that gives me as much shit as you do is okay in his book."

"Well, if that's the case, he and I will be besties by the time we come home. Now start at the beginning. I'm going to stand here and take it all in while I sip my coffee."

"Come sit," I invited as I reached over and patted the seat next to mine.

"Can't do it, little one. My ass is killing me."

"Let me get you a . . ."

"I already took some Tylenol, and I'm not drinking any more of your devil tea unless I feel the urge to sleep like the dead for hours. Talk to me."

"The short and simple story is that I married a man because my father made a business arrangement with my father-in-law. The two thought it would be a good idea to join our families. My mother-in-law was known to be a very clumsy and accident prone woman - at least, that's the story everyone stuck to. Everyone knew what was really going on, but no one wanted to admit that her husband was abusive. My husband learned how to treat a woman at the hands of his powerful father - a man he was dying to become. My father sold me into that life for his own personal gain. I fought him, but there was nothing I could do. By the time my brothers found out what was going on, it was too late. I was already married."

"Is your ex-husband still alive?"

"Yeah, but he's banished from the family just like I am. I'll get to that in a minute."

"Go ahead." Hook tipped his coffee mug toward me and unsuccessfully tried to erase the look of rage off of his face.

"I graduated early and went on to medical school. With money from my father and father-in-law, I opened a clinic. It was basically an urgent care center that was a front for their own personal medical clinic. I worked on men who'd been injured doing nefarious things - sewed up cuts from knife fights, took out bullets, set broken bones. I was miserable, and I hated everything about my life except my son. I raised him to know the difference between a real man and men like his father. I stayed because there was no way they'd ever let me see him if I left. Two days after his 18th birthday, I called a cab and had him drive me to the real emergency room where I confessed that my husband had beaten me, more than once, and gave the cops videos from the cameras I'd set up inside the house."

"And he was prosecuted."

"It was a slap on the wrist compared to what he put me through. But I'd done the unthinkable and gotten the cops involved and then he did the unforgivable and spilled some of their secrets. Because of my son, they let me live. They knew he'd never forgive any of them if something really happened to me, but I was banished, and they faked my death. I'm not allowed to visit because everyone there thinks I'm dead. I knew that someday I'd have to run, and I'd planned ahead. I skimmed money off the clinic for years and invested it through Frankie. If something happened to me, she would take care of my son. I left, but my brothers and their families kept in touch with me as much as possible. They sneak down to Texas and see me as often as they can without drawing any suspicion. Sometimes I meet them when they're vacationing or doing business somewhere. Hence the Vegas trip with my son in the fall."

"If your brothers and son know you're alive, why don't they stand up for you?"

"That's not our way, Hook. They're already putting themselves in jeopardy by talking to me. Someday, my father will die as will my father-in-law. When that happens, my brothers will make sure that my ex-husband pays for what he did and then he won't be a threat either. They're just biding their time until they're in charge of my family and my son is in charge of his father's family. Then the peace that the old men wanted will come to pass because they're going to work together. Either way, I'm dead, and I can't go back."

"So you're not going to run off and join the mob someday? You're going to stay here with me?"

"Is that what you want?"

"Yeah, little one, that's what I want."

The front door opened, and Hook and I both turned and watched Boss stroll into the house like he owned the place. He walked right up to my chair and pulled me into his chest for a tight hug. "I'm sorry I lost my temper and was an asshole to you. Thank you for fixing their fuck-up. I was pissed that they got their asses in a bind, and I was even more pissed that I found out about it later and couldn't do a damn thing to help. Jenn helped me realize that my hissy fit might have hurt your feelings when all you were doing was helping us."

"Hissy fit, huh?" Hook drawled.

"That's exactly what she called it when she chewed my ass this morning over breakfast and then again when I came home to check on her a few minutes ago. Now, I'm sorry I was shitty to you, and I'll try very hard not to do that in the future, especially when you're pulling bullets out of dumbasses who mean something to me."

"I'd like for the dumbasses to avoid getting shot, but if they do, I'll be there to take care of them, Boss."

"Thank you, Doc. I'm going to go back home to my old lady and rub her feet or something to make up for my shameful behavior." Boss's words said one thing, but the smile on his face told me that he was going to enjoy making it up to Jenn. Then his face changed, and he pointed his finger at Hook before he said, "We're meeting at the wellhouse this evening, and I want the details of everything that happened and just exactly how you boys got fucking shot."

"I'll be there," Hook assured him with a nod. "My woman and I are getting all our secrets out on the table, and I'll have to kindly ask you to get the fuck out of my house. We're almost to the part where I get to dry her tears and carry her to the bedroom so I can make her smile again."

"You want her to smile then drop your pants and let her laugh at you. Don't force the woman to participate in something she's gotta fake, man. That's cruel."

I couldn't help but laugh and then shook my head and sputtered, trying to defend Hook's honor somehow. "No, it's all good. I mean, he's good at . . . well, shit."

"I'll take your word for it, and I'll see you two later today. Doc, will you come hang with Jenn while we have our meeting?"

"Is that my name now? Some of the guys called me that last night."

"I do believe it's gonna stick."

"I like it. I'll visit with Jenn tonight, most definitely, Boss."

"See you brother. And I hope your ass hurts just because you're stupid."

"Yeah, It hurts," Hook assured him. "See you tonight."

We watched Boss walk out the front door, and I turned my attention back to Hook. "Where were we?"

"I was telling you that I want you here with me permanently."

"Hook, I want to be, but if there comes a time where I feel like your being with me puts you in danger, I'll have to leave you, and I won't say goodbye. That's why it's better if I'm alone."

"You're not alone anymore, little one. The big man who just busted in like he owns the place is proof of that. And the guys from last night along with the rest of them in the club . . . they're keeping you, sweetheart. Anyone that can stand up to Preacher having one of his fits and give him his shit right back to him is the right kind of people for us to have around. You're their Doc, and you're my little one."

"How bad does your butt hurt?"

"I can think of a few ways that you might be able to take my mind off the pain."

"So can I, and the one that's your favorite won't hurt your cute little butt at all."

"And which one do you think is my favorite?" Hook asked as I slowly walked around the bar. When I dropped down to my knees in front of him and yanked on his sweats, he laughed softly and said, "Top three, most definitely."

I put my mouth on him and took him all the way to my throat. I heard the coffee mug hit the bar right before he put his hands in my hair and held on for the ride. We'd see if this stayed in the top three or jumped up to the number one spot.

From the sounds he was making as he held onto my hair, I knew that right now, this was moving up the ranks.

13

HOOK

"Damn, I love what you've done with the place," Kitty said as he walked down the stairs into the cellar attached to Boss and Jenn's wellhouse. "So, this is our new meeting room."

"Looks good, Boss. I like it. How did this happen?" Bug asked from a few steps behind Kitty.

"I decided that we needed an official gathering place rather than all of you fuckers taking over my house. Now that Hook's got a woman, you don't need to be taking over his house either. I went and did a little shopping and found some furniture. Cap helped me decorate. He's got a flair."

"Obviously he learned it in prison," Santa said drolly as he looked at the white walls and cement floor.

"It's a work in progress. You guys find something you want to hang up, feel free. We've got a bar, a fridge, and chairs to sit in. What more do you want?" Captain asked the group as we all walked around and chose a place to sit down around the table at one end of the room.

"I like it. It has reinforced walls so no one can hear shit from the outside. We figured that out when we entertained our guest last month. It fits. The fact that it looks like a large prison cell makes it even more fitting," Preacher said as he looked around. "We need to get some of those cafeteria trays for the kitchen. I miss those. They kept my food separated."

"Let's talk about what happened last night," Boss started out after everyone was seated. "Going out and poking the bear was all fun and good until the bear shot you in the ass, huh?"

"We've been doing it for a while," I admitted.

"It's a whole lot of fun!" Captain chimed in. When Boss slowly turned his head and glared at him, Captain pulled his lips in between his teeth and slowly nodded his head.

"All of you have been doing this?"

"I never got to go," Bug grumbled. "Fucking work."

"It was for a good cause!" Preacher blurted. "We didn't spend a dime of that money on ourselves. We donated every dollar to good causes. It was my turn to choose next, and I was going to donate the money to this food truck that goes around and feeds the homeless."

"We can't do that anymore, guys," Boss told the group, making sure to look each of us in the eye

"But they're hungry," Preacher whined.

"We'll be more careful, Boss. I swear," Chef promised. I thought at any minute, he might start stomping his foot. He looked so much like a kid whose toy had been taken away. "I really liked getting to punch shitty people, and so did Hook."

"I really did, brother. I miss that."

"Then join a fucking gym and get into a ring," Boss growled. "As a matter of fact, that's on the agenda for discussion when Sin and his guys get here."

"It's just not as rewarding when you're hitting someone you like," Chef whispered as he looked down at the table. "They don't squeak the same."

Santa sighed and nodded in agreement. "He's right. In a gym, you don't get to chase them around either."

"Or tackle them!" Captain blurted. "That was fun too."

"Yes!" Chef agreed as the big man bounced in his chair.

"Can we at *least* go find the ones that shot us?" I asked Boss. I put my hands together and tried for my saddest face. "Please."

"It's like I'm surrounded by fucking children," Boss grumbled as he leaned back in his chair and stared at the ceiling. "Jesus. You guys need to get a fucking hobby."

"We *had* a hobby," Kitty mumbled before he rested his chin on his hand and stared at Boss with a forlorn expression. "It was a fun and productive hobby. Charities around town got money they needed while we exercised with cardio and boxing. We got to ride our bikes around, and we bonded while we were hunting. You can't get all that from a bowling league."

"We really need to figure out who brought guns to the party. That was so against the rules of the game."

"Cap, really? What am I supposed to do when my officers get a call about a disturbance and go find my club brothers beating the shit out of people?"

"Your officers should understand that they're not really people, Boss. They're drug dealers, " Santa argued. "Now, if we were sitting outside of the bingo hall waiting to beat the crap out of little old ladies, the cops would have a reason to arrest us. But we're not doing that."

"Technically, we're taking the trash out. We should be on the payroll," Kitty added. "If anything, we're helping your department."

"I just can't fucking deal with this shit right now. I've got cops on the actual payroll who are probably in league with the assholes you're beating on, and there's not a goddamn thing I can do about it without evidence. Then I've got you assholes getting shot and not even calling me to tell me what happened. I've got to find out when Sin comes over and interrupts me having fun time with my old lady."

"That's why you were so pissed!" I yelled as I slapped the table. "I knew there had to be a good reason!"

"How about the fact that my friends got fucking shot? That's a good fucking reason!" Boss yelled, and I knew I'd pushed too far.

"We'll be good," Chef promised. He sighed and leaned back in his chair. "Maybe we could start a softball team. That would be fun."

"We should do that. I'm one hell of a first baseman," Stamp boasted. "I played on a team in prison, and we kicked ass."

"They gave you bats in prison?" Boss asked, so shocked that he'd forgotten how pissed he was.

"It only lasted for a few games and then someone fucked it all up," Stamp admitted. "But when I was playing, I was awesome on first."

"I have to say that the snacks at your meetings are fantastic. This shit is so good. I hope Lyric gets the recipe," Sin said between bites of the bread pudding with chocolate sauce Brea and Paula had brought down a few minutes before.

They'd also left us a few carafes of caramel lattes and a fruit platter with dip. Apparently, none of the women up at the house understood we were bikers. We needed to eat shit with our fingers, gnaw meat off bones we held in our bare hands, growl and grunt between carnivorous bites and belch after we'd chugged a beer.

Instead, I was using a spoon to eat one of the best desserts I'd ever tasted, and I was doing it with a cup of designer coffee in front of me and a napkin in my lap.

What the fuck had our world come to?

"Okay, guys, not sure you'll be able to hear me over all the moaning you're doing, but let's get started," Boss addressed the group. Most everyone had a chair around the table, but a few others were seated at the bar and on the couches as they enjoyed their snack. "Sin's guys nabbed a guy this afternoon stealing mail from Paula's house. Problem was he was just a kid. Couldn't beat the information out of him, but they did tag him with a tracker before they let him go."

"That was my shit," Preacher boasted. "Tiny little fucker. I've got those things all over the place."

"How long will the tracker last? What's the battery life?" Phantom, one of the members of the AIMC asked.

"It's got a solar charger on it, bud. If it loses charge, it will come back on when it gets into a bright light. I've got some in my saddlebag if you want to take a look."

"Hell yeah," Phantom agreed with a nod. "That's cool as shit."

"They managed to get it onto his belt when they went looking for some ID. Kid goes to high school, but there's no record of siblings. Not sure what his connection might be. He insisted he just wanted to see if the box had something cool in it," Sin told our group. "We let him go, and Preacher is keeping a record of his movements for a while."

"Now, the question is will they stop using Paula's things to mail their shit now that we've popped one of them?" Torpedo asked.

"We'll keep an eye out for a while, but I'm betting they'll stop. With Preacher watching this kid, maybe we can figure out where he was taking the stuff he stole. And since you guys are camped out all over the place watching the other houses that were broken into, we'll either see that same kid or figure out there are others," Boss told our group. "There have been three more abductions, but they weren't here in town. All three happened close, but in different jurisdictions. My guess is that's been going on for a while, and no one ever made the connection. The women that were taken from the other towns were a little bit older and not quite as squeaky clean as the college girls that were snatched from around here."

"Shit. So the other cops probably don't even care," I mused. "Are there even active investigations?"

"Not really, no. But friends of two of the three insist that these ladies would never leave town without a word. They've got kids, man," Boss asserted.

"What else is going on in this fine city of ours?" Chef asked grumpily. "You know, if you'd let us hit people, we'd all feel a lot better about this shit."

"About that. My guys and I did a little recon today and found the guy that shot y'all along with the guys you were working over when it happened," Sin said with a wicked smile. "They're hog-tied in the back of Rampage's truck."

"You didn't!" Stamp said with a huge smile.

"They brought us gifts," Preacher said as he looked around the room. "That's a friendship right there, boys."

Sin laughed for a second and added, "My mom worked hard to teach me manners, and one of her lessons was never show up to a party empty-handed. It's the least we could do for you guys. We eat like kings every time we come over."

PAULA

"And you were a doctor?"

"Yes, Jenn. I was a doctor," I told her again. "Why is that so hard to believe?"

"You went to school for all those years and now you don't even use that knowledge?"

"How many degrees do you have again?" Brea asked from her spot on the other side of the bar. She had her head down and was concentrating on something she held in her lap. She'd been at it for a while and seemed frustrated. "I have two degrees. I was top of my class in charm school and graduated with degrees in veiled sarcasm and another in 'bless your heart'."

"I get the sarcasm, but I have to ask, what is the 'bless your heart'?"

"Well, Paula, it's like this." Brea fluffed her hair and leaned closer to us as she raised her eyebrows. Her accent was even thicker when she said, "Did you see Louisa at the grocery store today? Her hair was just a mess, and she'd put on weight. You know she caused quite the scandal when she left her husband for that younger man, and just look at her now. She's all alone and has nothing good to show for all those years of marriage. Bless her heart."

Jenn and I laughed and started snorting and wheezing when Brea added, "And I minored in 'God bless her'."

"Where I come from, we don't quite play it that way. It's more like . . ." I cleared my throat and channeled my best Brooklyn accent before I said, "Did you see that bitch looking at me? Did you see her? Oh, hell no."

"You sound like Marisa Tomei in *My Cousin Vinny*."

"Jenn's right. That impression was perfect," Brea agreed.

"That wasn't an impression, girls. I really sounded like that. It slips out now and then when I'm really mad or if I'm talking to my brothers, but I've learned to keep my accent pretty neutral over the years." Finally, I had to ask, "Brea, what are you doing over there?"

"I was putting in a load of laundry for these two, and these aprons are just tangled all to hell. I'm trying to get the knots out," Brea explained as she held up one of the aprons she was working on. "What the hell?"

"Um, you can just put those in the laundry basket, Brea," Jenn said quickly. "You don't, um, have to . . . Boss used those last night to, um . . ."

"I'm gonna throw up now," Brea said as she stood and held the aprons up with her fingertips as she walked toward the laundry room. "That is so gross. The two of you are just gross for sleeping with those two men anyway. I try so hard not to think about it, but shit like this happens, and I want to vomit."

"Oh, come on," I yelled after her, wondering if she could hear me all the way in the laundry room. "They're not all *that* bad."

"Gross," Brea reiterated when she walked over to the sink to wash her hands.

"Come on. I'll pick three. Out of Bug, Santa, and Kitty make your fuck, marry, kill selections."

I added, "You have to choose one for each category. No skipping."

"Fuck, marry, kill," Brea mused. "Santa, Kitty, and Bug, only because Bug is a smartass like me and Kitty is the quietest."

"Hmm. Okay, good reasons, I guess. Let me think." Then I threw out, "Captain, Chef, and Preacher."

Brea turned and stared at me for a second with fire in her eyes, and I knew I'd painted her into a corner.

"That one's too hard. I'd kill Captain because he's so grumpy all the time, and I'd kill Preacher because he won't shut up about shit."

"You've gotta choose," Jenn teased.

"If I can put a ball gag in Preacher's mouth then I guess Preacher, Chef and Captain."

"You'd marry Chef, huh?"

"Not in real life. I wouldn't marry any of them. I already lost one love, and I'm not ready to lose another one. People getting shot at would be enough to throw all of them out of the ring. No offense, Paula." Brea opened the refrigerator door and stood there for a second before she pulled out a jar of pickles. She opened it up and pulled two out before she tightened the lid and set the jar back in the refrigerator. "What about you? Jenn and Preacher told me that Hook said he loved you this morning. How'd that go over?"

I smiled wickedly and admitted, "I sucked the life force right out of his body and had him speaking in tongues for 10 minutes right there in the kitchen."

"That's my girl," Brea cheered and gave me a high five before she sat down across the table from me. "While he was a quivering mass of stupid, formerly known as my friend Hook, did you tell him you loved him right back?"

"I didn't. I want him to make sure that's really how he feels. It's only been a month, and he learned a lot about me recently. I want to give him time to process."

"For someone so cute, she sure is dumb," Jenn mused as she watched Brea devour the pickles with a disgusted look on her face. She looked at me and bluntly said, "You're dumb as a rock. I'm just saying."

"Yep."

"I'll tell him. When it's right, I'll tell him."

"Don't waste any chances, Paula. You never know when it will be too late."

14

HOOK

"I set more traps. I've got the four you caught in my truck. I'll get them all fixed up and bring them back to you once they're well," I told Pop, my mentor and father figure, the man who'd helped me adapt when I'd been paroled and become a free man for the first time in almost 20 years.

"I thank you, son. I was on my morning walk and realized there were twice as many cats around as there were before I got shot."

"You take someone with you on that walk?"

"I've got that damn walkie that Brea insists I haul around." Pop huffed as he touched the radio attached to his belt. "It's a sad day when a man can't walk his own property without having to check in like a child. And they won't fucking let me drive, son. You've gotta talk to them."

"Doctors said you can't drive yet, Pop. You know they all went to college for a long time and learned all this shit. They didn't get their medical license out of a Cracker Jack box and decide to start throwing out rules just to piss you off."

"A man doesn't get to be my age by following the rules."

"You almost didn't get to this age because you went off half-cocked chasing some idiot down in the middle of the night."

"Psh." Pop dismissed me with a wave.

"You gotta take care of yourself, old man. What would happen to us if we didn't have you to keep us on the straight and narrow?"

"You've got a woman to do that now, son. I'll focus on the other boys." I had to hold back a laugh when he called us boys. In the small group of men that made up our MC, I was the youngest, and I was past 40. Hell, I'd probably call everyone 'boy' when I was 80 years old too. "Where is that pretty little thing, anyway?"

"She had some errands to run and then she was going to see her friend who works at the hospital."

"Are you keeping a smile on her face?"

"I put one there every chance I get."

"Keep doing that. Once you stop is when it's over."

"Good advice. I'll follow it."

"If some of these other fools would get their heads out of their asses and see what's right in front of them, we could all be fat and happy."

"You got women picked out for all of us, huh?"

"Do you really think Boss would have bought a $5 cup of coffee if I hadn't encouraged him?"

"Maybe. How do you explain me and Paula?"

"Pretty woman like our Cool Cat's gonna have other

pretty women around her, don't you think?"

"The two of them have befriended Brea. Did you know that?"

"About time that girl got back in the game. I've got my eye on her and a plan in the works."

"Does she know this?"

"She's a damn sight more stubborn than all of you, so it might take some finesse, son. If I tell her what's going to happen, she'll just resist even harder."

"I'll sit back and enjoy the show."

'Buckle up, boy. It's going to be one hell of a ride. Now get those damn cats out of here and have the safe sex talk with 'em. Last thing I need to be is Lord of the Cats."

"Then stop feeding them, Pop. You quit putting out food, and they'll quit following you around like you're the pied piper."

"I'm not feeding them, son. They eat mice. I put that crunchy food out there for supplemental nutrition."

I laughed at him for a second and shook my head. We'd been having this conversation for years, and he wasn't likely to change. The man went through 30 pounds of cat food every week and bitched about it every time he refilled the bowls.

"I'm headed out. You call me if you need something, you hear?"

"I don't need shit except privacy and a knife to cut this

leash off that you kids seem to think I need around my neck."

"Bye, old man."

Pop didn't say anything else, just turned to walk over to the office, probably so he could boss some more people around and meet his quota for the day. I had to laugh when cats started coming from everywhere and followed him like a line of ducklings, waiting for him to show them some attention or give them food.

I looked around at the houses surrounding Pop's and let my eyes land on the one I'd lived in when I first got out of prison. It was the first time I'd had a space of my own in almost 20 years, and it was quite an adjustment getting used to making my own hours and cooking my own food. It was harder at night when things were quiet. Prison was never quiet, even in the dead of night. When I got out, I couldn't sleep without a fan on and the television blaring in the other room.

Another thing that helped me sleep was the sound of the traffic on the highway just outside the gates of Pop's little neighborhood. His businesses, the towing company, and the custom parts business were housed in a building a stone's throw from his front door. Behind all the homes he'd built for the ex-cons he helped were acres of junk cars people picked through for parts and pieces.

My eyes fell on the bar that had popped up next to the truck stop across the highway. I'd never been in there and could only imagine the clientele out here on the highway where the only people who stopped in were truck drivers and other people that lived their lives behind the wheel on the open road. As I watched, a few young men walked out of the bar and through a hole in the fence that led straight into the parking area where the semis sat while their drivers slept or took care of their business inside.

I shook off my thoughts and got into my truck. I needed to get these cats to the office so I could work on them today. Having the safe sex talk with them was how Pop described it, but there was much more involved when we trapped strays out here. It would take a few days to get them straightened out, but at least when I returned them to the fields they called home, they wouldn't end up making hundreds more babies in their lifetime.

I hit the button on my dash and tried to call Paula again. I'd left her in bed this morning, and she was gone when I'd shown up for lunch. She had quite a few things to do today and then we had a dinner planned with several of the guys. She'd gotten together with Stamp and planned out an authentic Italian menu, and I knew I wasn't the only one excited about dinner tonight.

I guessed that the guys would start trickling in anytime now, waiting around for a little of Paula's attention that they seemed to crave. There was just something about that woman's sharp wit and take-no-prisoners attitude that seemed to call to them.

Boss and I had found good women to add to our group, and I knew my brothers appreciated having them around all the time. I couldn't imagine what life would be like if the men I held closest to my heart didn't get along with the woman I'd decided to make a future with.

One would have to go, and it wouldn't be my brothers.

Paula didn't answer, so I called Jenn and Boss's to see if she happened to be there. When Jenn said she hadn't seen her all day, I started to get worried. It wasn't like Paula to ignore her phone or disappear without a word, especially since Jenn got her cast off today and would have one free arm. The girls had planned to celebrate by getting their nails done at the salon, and Paula had stood her up.

I tried to call again, and the phone just kept ringing until it connected to voicemail.

I was worried, but I'd give her another hour before I started freaking out. Maybe she got caught up somewhere and left her phone in the car. That had to be it.

"Why don't I smell bread? I was promised fresh bread, people," Preacher yelled as he walked through the front door to where I was sitting at the bar. "Where's Doc? She's supposed to be on the bread, dammit."

"She had some errands to run today, and she's running late getting back," I told him, but I couldn't keep the worry out of my voice as I glanced out the window hoping to see her headlights coming up the drive.

"How late is she?"

"She told me to meet her here at 2:30 so we could start the sauce and get the bread going. I haven't seen her, and she's not answering any of our calls."

"Well what the fuck are you doing sitting around? Why aren't you out there looking for her?"

"Where the fuck should I start, Preach? She had about 10 things to do today and could have gotten caught up at any one of them. It's just now 6:00."

"Is she ever late?"

"Not usually?"

"Is she the type to go back on her word?"

"No."

"Let me get my computer."

"What's your computer going to help?"

"Mind your business, Stamp. Make me some food. I skipped lunch so I'd have plenty of room tonight," Preacher called as he walked toward the door. The man had more computers and laptops than I could count, and he was never without one or even two in his saddlebags.

"What the fuck does he want with his computer? Is he tracking her?" I asked Stamp when Preacher was outside.

"Probably. He's probably got trackers on all of us. For a man who is positive that we're all being watched, he seems intent on doing that himself."

"Did you ever take that tracker off her Expedition?"

"No. I never even thought about it again. I guess you didn't either," Stamp said as he pulled his phone out of his back pocket and started scrolling through his contacts. He put the phone up to his ear, and I heard him greet Phantom and ask, "How long do those trackers you put on cars work? Can you look for that one you loaned me? Doc's out of pocket, and we're starting to get worried. Okay, call me back when you find it. Thanks, man." Stamp put his phone down on the counter and went back to the sauce he had simmering on the stove. "He'll call when he gets to his computer. He said it should still be active."

"What's Preach doing on the porch?" Boss asked as he and Jenn walked into the house. Jenn's dog came trotting in and plopped down next to Tonya. She put her big paw over him and pulled him close for a snuggle and within seconds, the dog's eyes were closed. "I asked him and he shushed me, the fucker."

Jenn glanced over at the bedroom and around the house before she asked, "Where's Paula?"

"I guess that's what Preach is doing with his computer. Paula's still not answering, and she hasn't shown up. I'm trying to keep a level head, but it's not really working out for me. How's the hand, Jenn?"

"Stiff and swollen. I was going to ask her about that," Jenn told me. She looked as worried as I felt when she said, "It's not like her to just disappear. She knew we were coming over for dinner, and when I talked to her this morning, she said she'd be home by lunch."

"I'm gonna call Frankie," Stamp said as he picked his phone back up. "Shit. You call her, Hook. I don't want to miss Phantom's call or have to cut it short with Frankie when he beeps in."

I pulled my phone out of my pocket just as Jenn said she was going to call and check with Brea to see if she'd seen her today.

I dialed Frankie's number, and when she picked up, she was out of breath. I didn't beat around the bush. "Paula's not answering her phone, and she's not made it home."

"She told me she was going to start making pasta right after lunch, Hook. She should have been home all day."

"She's not here. Hold on," I said as I stood up and walked toward my bedroom for some privacy. When I was alone in the room, I pressed her. "She said that if she thought I was in danger, she'd leave without saying goodbye. Did she do that, Frankie? Be honest."

"No, Hook. She didn't. We have a plan in place for that, and she hasn't put that in motion."

"You have a plan for that? Seriously?"

Frankie was quiet for a minute before she sighed and said, "Yes, Hook. We do. If she was going to vanish, she'd have to tell me because I'm the one that would need to pull the trigger for her. I've got what she needs to disappear."

I sat down on the bed and leaned forward as I stared at the floor and processed what Frankie was telling me. Paula had an out if she needed one. In the six weeks since she'd told me about her past and we'd agreed we were going to stay together, she hadn't told Frankie she wouldn't need to leave. She was still keeping her options open.

"She wouldn't leave you, Hook. There's no way. We've had this plan since the day she moved in with me years ago. Just because the option's there doesn't mean she'd take it. Her brothers and I have people in place who will give us some warning if something bad is headed this way. That's how she'd know to run - I'd call her, and I haven't called her,

Hook. I promise."

"Do you think she'd leave me?"

"No. I don't. I think she'd fight it out and do whatever it took to stay with you. I'm going to swing by my house and make sure she's not there for some reason. If I find her, I'll call you. If she's not there, I'll head to your place. I'm sure it's just a misunderstanding. She got her times mixed up or something."

"Frankie, if she ever tries to pull that cord and get shit started, will you tell me? I know she's your friend . . ."

"I'd like to say she's my friend, and I'd never do that, but I would, Hook. You're what she needs to have that life she's only dreamed about. If I helped her throw that away, I wouldn't be any kind of friend at all."

"Thanks, Frankie. I'll see you in a bit."

Frankie hung up, and I sat there on the edge of the bed trying to get myself under control. I had a horrible feeling and needed to do something, anything, to find Paula. I dialed her number again, and this time, it went to voicemail after the first ring. Either the battery had gone dead, or someone had turned it off.

"Fuck."

Stamp called out, "Phantom's got her car!" at the same time that Preacher flew through the front door and exclaimed, "I found her!"

I jumped up and hurried into the living room. Stamp was on one end of the house with his phone to his ear, and

Preacher was standing by the front door holding his laptop.

"Well, where is her car? Where is she?" I yelled.

"The old base," Preacher said softly. "She's right in the middle of the old base out past No Man's Land behind Pop's place."

"That's what Phantom said," Stamp confirmed.

"She's got no reason to be out there," I told them.

"Tell Phantom to call Sin to see if he and his men can meet us here," Boss ordered Stamp. "I'll text the rest of the guys."

"What's No Man's Land?" Jenn whispered.

"It's a neighborhood you don't visit unless you're wearing body armor or you want to buy drugs," Boss explained in a calm voice. "It's nowhere that Paula needs to be."

15

PAULA

Kelli, my contact at the licensing and permit office, flipped through my paperwork before she tilted her head with a curious look on her face. "You've been doing month-to-month for years. What changed?"

"I've always wanted to keep my options open in case I felt the need to move on, but things have changed. I'm here permanently now."

"Oh, something changed, she says." Kellie teased as she typed a mile a minute. "It's a boy, isn't it? It's always a boy."

Considering that Kelly was at least 60, I didn't know if she was calling a man my age a boy because she considered him young enough to be her son or because she thought it was cute. I decided on cute and rolled with it. "It does have to do with a person of the male persuasion, yes."

"Like I said, it's always a boy. Well, I guess it could be a girl. To each their own," she added before she spun her chair around and held her arm out waiting for my permit to come out of the printer behind her desk. "I guess I won't see you until this time next year then."

"Come to one of the craft fairs and visit with me. My friend owns the S'mores coffee truck. I'll buy you a cup."

"I might take you up on that. I love her desserts!"

Kelli stamped the paper she'd just printed and folded it precisely before she slipped it into a clear protector for me to display at my booth. "There you go! You can come back in 11 months and renew for the next year."

"Okay, I'll see you then. Thanks for all your help, Kelli."

"My pleasure. You be good, honey. I'm glad you decided to stay here in Tenillo."

I stood up and followed Kelli out of her office and walked into the foyer while she veered off to call the next person in line.

Once I was in my truck, I tossed my purse into the passenger seat and started the engine. I was twisted around in my seat looking for traffic before I pulled out of my parking space when I felt someone come up beside me between the two seats. I grabbed for the door handle so I could jump out, traffic be damned, when I heard a man's voice say, "I'll shoot you in the fucking head before your feet hit the ground."

I let go of the door handle and turned back toward the steering wheel when the voice told me in the same menacing voice, "Pull out and drive straight until I tell you to turn. If you try anything, I'll fucking kill you."

"Got it." I twisted around and waited for a gap in traffic and then pulled out onto the street. "Why are you kidnapping me? I'm just curious."

"I'm the delivery man. Drive."

"Oh, so whoever's calling the shots isn't going to stick their neck out and kidnap me in broad daylight. They sent you in case you get caught. That makes sense."

"Shut up and drive."

"I've never understood the thought process of the evil minion," I said conversationally as if I was just out for a casual drive with one of my friends. "You do what you're told and assume all the risks while the evil ruler sits in his cave somewhere waiting for you to bring him a new toy. Is that how it works?"

"I told you to shut up."

"I talk when I'm nervous. I haven't seen your gun, but I'm going to assume that it would hurt if you shoot me with it, so I'm nervous. Understandable, right?" I glanced in the rearview mirror and saw not one man in the back but three. One I could possibly handle, two was a crapshoot, but three was damn near impossible. Shit. "Wow. The evil ruler sent three of you for little old me? I'm flattered."

"You're going to be dead if you don't shut the fuck up," a second voice told me.

"Honestly, you're going to kill me anyway, so why should I listen to you? I watch enough TV to know that if you let me see your faces, I'm not going to live through this little adventure."

"Adventure," the third voice repeated before he laughed. "Oh, you're going to have an adventure alright, but not until the boss gets through with you. Your man and his friends took something important to us, and we're going to take something important to him."

"He took your girlfriend? That doesn't seem like

something he'd do."

"Shut up," Minion Number One growled. "Turn right at the light and get on the loop to go around town."

"What did he take?"

"I told you to shut up, bitch," Number One said

"If it wasn't your girlfriend, was it your dog? I can see him taking your dog, especially if you're mean to it or something." I rambled trying to figure out which of the three was the weak link. I guessed it was the first guy, which was disturbing because he was closest to me and had a gun. He kept taking the bait and repeating himself, and I could tell by the volume and tone of his voice that I was getting to him by disobeying his orders.

The other two just looked menacingly at my reflection in the rearview mirror. Minion Number Two kept glancing at Number Three. That meant that Three was the one in charge. If I could, I'd kill him first and leave the other ones confused. It would make them easier to pick off.

"Where are you three goons taking me? It is like a big compound full of baddies? Which TV show should I be imagining here? It's Tenillo, so I'm guessing something rustic. Maybe a barn? Oooh, I know. You're taking me to an abandoned farmhouse. Am I close?"

"Get off on Honesty, and take a right."

"I do not get off on honesty. If you knew me at all, you'd understand how laughable that is," I said under my breath as I put on my blinker and slowed down on the exit ramp. "Do your mothers know what you do for a living? My son dabbles in criminal shit, and I'm just gonna say, it's worrisome. Your mothers are probably worried about you, you know."

"Shut. Up." Minion Number Three had gotten his fill of my shit and was starting to crack. Number Two looked nervous. Unfortunately, I couldn't see Number One's face, so I wasn't sure if he was more pissed off or nervous. "Turn into that gap in the fence."

"I don't want to offroad in this. I just had my suspension . . ."

"Turn into the gap in the fucking fence!" Number Three was yelling now. I'd pushed a little too much. I tended to do that. "Go into the open bay and put the truck in park. Jesse, get the bitch out and gag her. I am not listening to anymore of her fucking shit. Throw her in the office and keep her there until I talk to the guys. There's no fucking way anyone will take her unless we cut her goddamn tongue out first. Jesus Christ."

"I didn't mean to make you angry when I talked about your mom," I said as I held the man's eyes in the mirror. "But I'm sure she's worried about you."

I put the Expedition in park and sat there waiting for the men to pile out. Finally, Jesse, or Minion Number One as I preferred to think of him, opened my door and yanked me out by my hair. I went willingly as he dragged me over to a big metal building toward a room that was built on the side. I heard the big doors roll down behind us, and when I tried to look around, Jesse jerked on my hair.

Since I couldn't look behind me, I studied the area in

front of me. There were long tables set in neat rows with yellow bubble wrap envelopes lined up on them with small baggies of trinkets and things scattered around.

"Are we crafting? I just went to my favorite bead store and stocked up. The boxes are in the back of my truck. I'll get them out later if you want and show you how to make this really neat . . ."

Jesse shook me by my hair so hard that my feet came off the ground, and I stumbled into him, knocking him off course right before he stopped in front of the office door. He pulled out a ring of keys and chose one before he slipped it into the lock and then pushed me into the room. He slammed my face down on the desk and yanked my arms up behind my back. I felt him start to wrap tape around my wrists, so I balled up my fists to make my forearms bigger and give myself wiggle room. When he was finished, he wrapped some more tape around my boots at my ankles and then slapped a piece over my face.

Finally, with his work done, he tossed me over to the side and was out of the office before I'd even bounced twice on the hard floor. He slammed the door behind him, and I heard him use the key to lock the deadbolt.

I wiggled my face around until the tape loosened and then worked my tongue out of my mouth and licked as much of the tape as it would reach. After less than a minute, it was hanging off my face, and I could take a full breath.

"Fucking amateurs," I scoffed as I twisted my body around and got into a sitting position. I worked at stretching the tape on my hands while I wiggled my feet inside my boots. By the time the tape was loose enough, I had one of my boots off, so my legs were more or less free. I bent forward at the waist and pulled my hands down around my ass and shimmied until they were behind my knees. Finally, I stepped back through the circle my arms made and pulled my hands up quickly toward my waist and broke the tape holding them together. "Fucking serious amateurs. Good Lord. They must have failed Kidnapping 101 in minion school."

I pulled the tape off my boots and wadded it into a ball before I reached down into my left boot and found the hidden compartment I'd fabricated. Once I had it ripped open, I pulled out two of the little tools my brother Vincente had given me. He gifted me an entire box of them before I moved to Texas. I slipped one over each index finger and flexed my hands for a second to get used to the feel of the rings. I reached down into my other boot and pulled out the thin knife I'd hidden in the lining and then pulled both boots back on. It wouldn't do to hurt my toes if I had to kick some fucker's nuts up into his throat.

It took me just a second to see that the deadbolt only unlocked with a key from the outside, so I was stuck in here until someone came to get me, or I broke the window and tried to make a run for it.

I was *not* a runner by any means, so I'd need to settle in and fight. I took stock of the office around me and moved things around so they'd be handy if I needed them. The chair that was in the corner was sturdy enough for me to stand on, so I pushed it over at an angle next to where the door would stop when opened.

With all the prep work done that I could do for now, I searched the office for a phone or fax - anything that I could use to send a message. I didn't find anything except a few granola bars in the desk. After taking some precious time searching for a best by date, I decided to eat one now and save one in my pocket for later.

I walked over to the window that looked out into the big building to see how many men were milling around. I didn't see a single one. They'd tied the mouthy woman up and neutralized her so they could do whatever minion shit they did in their time off.

Seriously. Amateurs.

I didn't have any way to tell time, but I knew by how badly I had to pee that I'd been here for hours already with only occasional signs of life outside in the warehouse. I knew I couldn't hold it much longer. Just to be a bitch, I got the coffee cup off the shelf behind the desk and squatted over it and peed.

I knew I was right there on the edge of hysteria when I had a flashback to peeing in a cup and finding out I was pregnant with Zacharia. What a thing to think about when you were being held hostage and pissing in some man's #1 Dad mug.

"Hook knows you're missing, and he's going to find you," I said softly to reassure myself. "He knows you were supposed to be home cooking. When he gets there and realizes you haven't made it, he'll call out the badass biker cavalry. He's going to find you, Paula. Have faith in your man."

I heard movement in the warehouse, so I carefully set my cup full of pee back on the shelf with a smile. Even if they killed me and threw my body in a ditch somewhere, I'd linger here in the office for a long, long time. I hurriedly buttoned my jeans and went back to my post at the edge of the window.

There were eight men out there now, and they broke off into sets of two. Each pair carried a long wooden box with rope handles. They all filed out of the warehouse, and I lost sight of them. I turned back and studied the room they'd come from. As I watched, more men came out carrying smaller wooden crates.

"They had all those men and shit in that little office? What the hell? Do they have some sort of evil minion portal in there or what?"

Once all the men had filed out, the warehouse was quiet again. I could see my truck. It still had the driver's door open from when Jesse the Asshole had yanked me out. I wondered if my purse was still inside and how many missed calls I had from Hook by now.

The sun was setting, and I was sure he was searching for me. Maybe the men had forgotten I was here, or maybe they didn't plan on doing anything with me until morning. I'd just decided to break the window and haul ass to my truck when I saw Jesse walking across the dark warehouse toward this office.

"Shit. Shit. Shit." I chanted as I hopped up on the chair and prepared myself. He'd been walking alone, so I'd have to assume there weren't any other men with him, but they could be on the way.

Jesse's keys rattled, and I heard the lock turn over right before he pushed the door open. He was three steps into the office before he realized I wasn't where he'd dropped me. As he turned his head to look around the door, I stuck my knife in his eye as hard as I could and pushed him to the side, closing the door with a thump as I pushed into him.

"Holy shit! It worked!" I hissed as I jumped up and stared down at the man on the floor. "And Dad said I never listened when he tried to teach me things!"

I yanked the knife out of Jesse's eye and threw up in my mouth a little as I wiped it off on his jeans before I slipped it back down into the lining of my boot. I checked his pockets and found two phones - an iPhone and a piece of shit burner.

"Fuck! What's his phone number?" I whispered frantically. "Shit!"

I dialed Frankie's cell and prayed she wasn't on duty and could answer. Hell, I didn't even know if she'd even answer an unknown number.

"Hello?"

"Frankie. Thank God. That old base out at the edge of town. The second big warehouse from the fence closest to the loop on the town side, not the country side of the place."

"Got it. You okay? Hook knows where you are, they're on their way. I'll text them."

"I have to hide. There are men everywhere, and I don't know how long I'll be alone. I'll call back when I can."

I hung up on Frankie and hit a few buttons to make sure both phones were silenced before I dragged the chair back over into the corner where it had been before. I crawled into the big box I'd emptied earlier and pulled everything in on top of me that I'd taken out of it. Once I'd arranged the stuff over me, I reached out with one hand to grab the string of tape I'd secured to the flap. I pulled it so that it folded over the box and then peeled it off in case someone actually looked inside.

I'd be fine here for a while. If anyone came in, they'd assume I escaped through the unlocked door and go searching for me. I just had to have faith that Hook and the guys would find me before anyone else did.

16

HOOK

I looked down at the screen when my phone vibrated and saw that I had a text from Frankie.

> *P called. 2nd bldg on the NW corner by gap in fence. Small office. Hiding now.*

"She's okay for now. She found a phone and called Frankie. She's hiding," I told Sin through the earbuds he'd given me. "She's in an office in the second building on the northwest corner by a gap in the fence."

"Confirm, building number two?"

"Yes."

"Stand by," Sin's voice came over the headphones.

"I want to go in there, Boss."

"We wait. They did this shit for years and were damn good at it considering they're all alive. Let them do their thing."

"Fuck," I hissed as I picked up the night vision binoculars and watched Sin and his men scurry around the buildings, darting here and there as they hid in the shadows. I watched four men go inside the building Frankie had described while the other men of the AIMC stayed outside, spread all over the place waiting for word.

"Target acquired," Saint said over the line. "Rendezvous Alpha."

"They got her?" Preacher asked from a few feet away. We were camped out in Pop's junkyard watching the men go in after Paula with equipment Sin had given us. As I watched, the men started moving again, but this time they were going past the building toward the loop. "Fuck. Which one was Alpha?"

"They're going across the loop where Stamp's waiting with the truck," Boss explained.

"I see her!" I whispered as I watched Paula running across the highway between two men. There were two more behind her and another two going slowly, pulling up the rear to watch their backs until Paula was safely away. I watched someone pick Paula up and toss her in the back of the truck before he climbed up into the bed with her. The other men did the same before Stamp slowly pulled out onto the highway and headed west.

"All clear. Call it in," Sin's voice came over the line, and it sounded like he was laughing. "Doc says it's about goddamn time."

"Hey, Chelsea. It's Boss. That stolen vehicle I called in earlier? We got the LoJack info on it, and I've got a location. It's out at the old base. I think Wrecker's on duty tonight. If you could have him get some guys together, I'd appreciate it." Boss was quiet for a few seconds and then said, "Tell him to give me a call if he needs me, and I'll come out. I'm not too far away from there right now."

Boss hung up and Wrecker's phone rang. He took the

call and started walking toward his patrol car as he gave the dispatcher instructions so they could assemble a team to safely retrieve Paula's car from the old base.

He and Boss had already decided which officers to call in, hoping that the ones they'd chosen were some of the good ones in case they found something at the base they could investigate legally. Sin and Wrecker had originally pushed to have the cops be the ones to storm the place and find Paula, but I'd reminded them that she didn't need to be on any reports that listed her name - especially if there would be some defense attorney trying to rip her apart on the witness stand.

"Ride out of here steady like you don't have a care in the world, brother," Preacher reminded me as I threw my leg over my bike to go to my woman. "We're right behind you."

PAULA

"Jesse?" I heard a man yelling from somewhere in the warehouse. "What the fuck are you doing in there, man?"

"You better not be sampling the goods. He wants her body clean when we drop her in the tiger cage," I heard another man say.

I didn't recognize either voice. I thought these must be different minions than the ones who'd been in the backseat earlier.

"Man, what the fu . . . "

I heard four faint pinging noises followed by two loud thumps.

"Fuck! Dead guy. No Doc." It was a voice I recognized.

"Saint? Don't shoot me," I whispered as I sat up in the box.

Saint spun around and looked at me in shock. "Hey there, pretty lady. Need a ride home?'

"Yes, please," I told him as he pulled me to my feet.

"You injured? Can you run?"

"Not usually, but I bet I can outrun you tonight."

"Target acquired," I heard Sin say from right outside the door. "Rendezvous Alpha."

"Come on, babe." Torpedo reached for my hand and pulled me out the door. The rest of the guys surrounded us, and we hurried out the side door and then hid in the shadows for a few seconds before Torpedo pulled me again. We ran through the gap in the fence and across the highway. Torpedo was on one side of me and Saint on the other. I recognized Stamp's truck and started to go around to the passenger door, but Torpedo picked me up and tossed me over the side and jumped in right behind me. "Lay down and make room, Doc. All of us gotta fit."

I slid over to the side wall of the truck bed and watched as the other five men piled in. It was a tight fit, so I pushed up and moved over on top of Torpedo. He wrapped his arms around me and scooted over close to the side so the

CEE BOWERMAN

other men could have more room. Stamp started driving and within seconds, we were up to the speed limit.

"It's about goddamn time you showed up! I thought you guys were never going to fucking get there. That was so fucking awesome. I'm a ninja now, too, right? I want some clothes like yours. I can barely see any of you back here. Are you wearing makeup?"

All the guys were laughing, and I heard Sin say, "All clear. Call it in. Doc says it's about goddamn time."

"It's not makeup, Doc."

"You spread it on your face to change your appearance, Saint. That's makeup. Women do it every fucking day, but our stuff doesn't turn us full ninja."

"You are just a little badass, aren't you?" Torpedo asked me with a laugh that shook my whole body. "Not phased even a little bit."

"You stuck that guy through the eye. What did you use?"

"The knife I keep in my boot," I explained. "Now I have to buy new jeans *and* a new pair of boots. I tried to wipe all the blood and tissue off my knife, but I know I missed some, and now it's down inside these boots. I'll never be able to wear them again because that's all I'll be able to think about. It's very unsanitary."

"What the fuck did you just cut me with if the knife's in your boot?" Saint asked.

"Oh shit! I'm sorry!" I held my hand up, not that he

could see it very well with only the lights from the poles above us zipping by at 70 miles an hour. "My brother gave me a box of these and made me promise never to leave the house without two, so I have hidden compartments in my shoes and bras to hold them. I had the knife in my boot, too, but that was just sort of an added thing."

"Are those rings with razor blades on them?" Pitbull asked as he held his hand out toward me. I pulled one of the rings off my finger and handed it to him. He held it close to his face and inspected it for a second before he said, "I'll be damned. You could slice the shit out of someone with these things."

"You certainly can. Especially if you punch them. You just slice through their skin like butter. I have one in my desk at home that I use to open my Amazon packages," I admitted. "I keep another one in the kitchen. I asked my brother to figure out how to get me some more. I thought I could pass them out to the girls as sort of a fucked-up Christmas gift or something."

"You are one twisted little lady, Doc. If things don't work out with you and Hook, give me a call," Pitbull said with a grin. "I could use a woman like you in my life."

"Nope. He's the one for me. You found me too late, buddy."

"That's the story of my life."

HOOK

"We're out of here, man."

"Sin, I can't thank you guys enough. Anything you ever need . . ."

"Our pleasure, Hook. We don't get to play around with the cool toys in the dark much anymore. And we don't mind at all since it ended up with us drinking your cold beer and watching your woman fall asleep in your lap like she doesn't have a care in the world."

"She was crashing from the adrenaline, and I made her eat a bite of one of her edible things," I admitted. "She's dead to the world, but I can't seem to make myself let go of her."

"I understand that. Hold her tight. We'll be in touch tomorrow when Wrecker has a report on what they found there. With everything she told us, I think we've got the mail situation figured out. I snagged her purse on our way out so she won't have to wait to get it out of evidence. It's on the table by the front door."

"Again, thank you is not enough. You and your guys have got all my respect, brother. We never could have snuck in like you did. There would have been bullets flying everywhere. You got out of there with none the wiser."

"Well, there were those two we dropped right before we found her."

"The rest of us are going, too, Hook. Tonya's in her room with the door shut. She's been fed and watered and I let her out to potty about an hour ago. Have Paula call me tomorrow when you finally let her out of bed."

"Thanks, Brea. You're the shit, woman."

"I know. Oh, one more thing in the kitchen and then I'm out," Brea said as she walked back toward the bar.

I watched Sin and his men file out along with Stamp and Preacher who'd stayed with us after everything calmed down. Paula moved around on my lap, and I realized she was probably uncomfortable and would feel better once she was in bed.

"Brea?"

"Yeah?" Brea called out from behind me in the kitchen.

"Will you turn down my bed? I want to lay her down so she can get comfortable."

"On it. Head that way."

I stood up from the couch with Paula in my arms and carried her to the bedroom. Brea had the covers folded to the side already, and she moved to the wall to turn off the light. I laid Paula down, and she instantly turned over onto her side with a sigh and pulled her legs up so that she was curled into a ball. Once she was covered up with the sheet and blanket, I walked over toward the door and followed Brea out. The two of us slid the doors closed so Tonya couldn't get in and bother Paula before I walked down the hall to let the cat out of her room while Brea went back to the kitchen.

Tonya and I walked down the hall and came out by the pantry. I saw Brea wiping off the counters one last time before she left.

"Thank you for taking care of us tonight, B."

"I'm not a commando, so I couldn't very well do anything else," Brea answered before she smiled over her shoulder at me. "You think she's going to be okay with all this? She seemed to handle it like a champ until the adrenaline crashed, and she got tired and shaky."

"She handled everything better than I ever imagined she would. It's like she knew exactly what to do in there. Fucking incredible, if you ask me."

"I get that she can think on her feet, but how did she know to do all that under stress? I couldn't have dealt with things nearly as well as she did. If I could have gotten out of the tape, I probably would have busted the window and tried to make a run for it. She sat there waiting like . . . well, like a big cat waiting on her prey to come closer."

"Preacher asked her almost the same thing you're thinking. She said if she'd broken the window and gotten out somehow, she wouldn't have had anywhere to go out in the middle of nowhere and she didn't have her phone. She waited on the guy to unlock the door so it would look like she escaped and then she hid right there in the room. That way, if someone found that fucker's body, they'd fan out and search for her outside the building and she could get to her car and haul ass toward town."

"Solid plan. Ballsy. Took a lot of quick thinking to come up with a strategy like that under so much stress. I'm glad it worked out for her, but I still want to know how she knew what to do and why her brother thought it was important that she carry fucking razor blades around all the time."

"Maybe there's some threat of being kidnapped when you're a mafia kid. Fuck, I don't know. I'll damn sure ask her that and more when she wakes up."

"I seriously want to go home and have Sis truss me up just so I can see if I can get my hands from the back to the front without detaching my arms at the shoulder," Brea said before she laughed softly. "My kid will probably video me rolling around on the floor and put it on fucking TikTok or some shit."

"I'd pay to see the video. Really. Next time we get together for beer or something, we'll have to fake a kidnapping and see if any of us can get out of the tape she had on her."

"Are you okay, Hook? You are much calmer than I would be if something like this happened to someone I love."

"I am so fucking far from okay, there's no way to measure it. First I was worried when she wasn't home when I thought she'd be, then I was terrified she'd left without a goodbye, and then I realized she'd been kidnapped and might die before we got to her. I'm not sure I'll ever be able to let her out of my sight again."

"You'll have to, though. Holding her down would be like wrapping your hand around a firecracker, Hook. You'd end up needing surgery to reattach your limbs. It wouldn't end well at all."

"You're exactly right. I'm going to have to fight the urge to hover. Maybe she'll give me a little time to recover first. I fully intend on keeping her naked in bed beside me for at least the next two or three days anyway. I already called

Linda and told her I was going to be unavailable for anything but major emergencies until Monday."

"I'm sure Boss and the guys will have to bother you two, but I'll stay away until she calls. I've got some jobs with Jenn's truck over the next few days, so I'll be busy anyhow. Right now, I'm going to go home to fall into bed. It's been a stressful evening, to say the least."

"Do you know how much I love you, Brea? You're one of the best friends I've ever had, and I couldn't live without you."

"Shit," Brea swore before she threw herself at me and gave me a strong hug. I'd barely squeezed her back when she pulled away and spun around. As she was hurrying to the front door, she called out over her shoulder, "I love you, too, man. Go get in bed with your woman. I'll talk to you soon."

I watched my friend leave and wished she could have what I'd found with my little one. I decided then and there to make sure she found it just like Boss and I had. If anyone deserved love, it was Brea.

Whether she wanted it or not.

17

HOOK

I heard Paula moving around in the bathroom, and a few minutes later, felt her crawl into bed and snuggle up to my side with a sigh. Her skin was cool, and I could smell her shampoo, so I assumed she had been up for a while and showered without me even realizing she was gone.

I opened one eye and realized it was bright around the edges of the curtains. I'd woken up with Tonya around dawn, fed her, and put her out in her day pen before I showered and came back to bed for more sleep. I'd tossed and turned last night thinking of all the ways things could have turned out differently, but when I came back to bed early this morning, I'd apparently slept like the dead.

"Are you awake?" Paula whispered.

"I am," I told her as I slid my arm under her pillow and wrapped it around her back. "How are you doing this morning? Did you get enough sleep?"

"I'm doing fine. I had an awesome night's sleep, and I'm refreshed and perky now."

"Perky?"

"How are you?" Paula whispered as her hand trailed down my belly and wrapped around my cock. I instantly started to harden, and she laughed softly before she said, "You're feeling perky too, huh?"

"Is that what we're calling it now?"

"Works for me. You feel like breakfast?"

"If it's you I'm eating, I'm famished," I told her as I pulled her body up and over mine. "You know how I like my breakfast, babe."

Paula pushed up and straddled my hips as she smiled down at me. "You know I love it when you have me for breakfast."

I reached up and cupped her heavy breasts before I gently pushed them together as I rubbed my thumbs over her hard nipples.

"God, you're beautiful, baby."

"You make me feel beautiful, Hook," Paula whispered as she covered my hands with her own. "I know you want to talk about what happened last night, but can we shelve that for a while? I just want to be here with you right now. No outside world. Just us."

"I can do that, little one. Anything for you. Now crawl up here and feed your man."

"Can I ask you some questions yet?"

"I suppose," Paula said before she sighed. "It's inevitable."

"How did you know all that shit? How to get out of the tape? How to set up the situation so you had the upper hand? All of it?"

"When I was a little kid, there was a disagreement between my family and another family that was in the, well, the same line of work as my father. Anyway, things were tense, and my father did something to piss off the head of the other family. He sent four men to our house while it was just my mom and I at home, and they took us away. They kept us in a small cabin by this lake for over a week."

"Holy shit. So this wasn't the first time you'd been kidnapped. How old were you?"

"I was 7 years old the first time. So, yes - this was my second time on this fucked-up ride."

"What in the hell happened?"

"At first, we were tied up, but when they got to the cabin and everything was secure, they let us free. We had full run of the place. Honestly, it was like a mini-vacation with just me and my mom. She was terrified, obviously, but I was pretty clueless. They treated us well. We had plenty of food, and there was a television and a shelf full of books. There was even a cabinet full of board games. We played a different one every afternoon while we were there. It was actually their family cabin that they frequented during the summer."

"And they just kept you there."

"For nine days. They were doing it to make Dad sweat, I guess. I've never really known what started the feud or the motive for the kidnapping, but they came to an agreement, and we were returned to my dad. They dropped us off at home like we'd just been their guests or something. That sent my dad and uncles into a tailspin. They were adamant that me, my mom, and everyone else in the family learn how to defend ourselves in case this ever happened again and we weren't as lucky the next time."

"Your dad taught you how to do all the things you did last night?"

"Well, he helped on occasion, but it was mainly three of his men that taught us everything they knew about how to escape from a kidnapper."

"And how did they come to have that skill set?"

"Because they worked for my dad and that was what they did for him. They took people places they didn't want to go and either held them there or got rid of them for my dad. They taught us how to survive by putting us through a mock kidnapping and talking us through how to get out of certain situations. I learned how to use what was around me as weapons, how to pick locks on doors and handcuffs, how to breathe quietly, and hide in plain sight. Just like last night. I hid in a box that was right there in the office. I made sure it looked just like it had when I'd walked in so they'd have no reason to even look in my direction. I could have stayed there for a long time, and no one would have even known."

"Holy shit. What a fucking thing to have to learn."

"I was just a kid, and it was mostly a game to me. It went on for years until something else happened when I was 12, and they sent me away to boarding school. My dad and another family got crossways. They came to an agreement and it included me, but I didn't get kidnapped that time."

"How did the agreement include you?"

"To help the two families unite and find peace, the men in charge ordered that I marry my ex-husband. They decided that three days before I turned 12."

"You're fucking kidding me."

"Nope. It was a well-kept secret. Even my brothers were clueless. I tried to refuse, but Dad explained that it was either me or my mom who had to go. I could get married and stay alive, or they could take my mom's life for payment. I chose marriage."

"And that's why you have to be dead now? Because you broke that agreement?"

"That's right. My son will take over for his grandfather when the time comes and things will be less tense. I still won't be able to go home or take my old name back, but I can quit looking over my shoulder like I have been since I left my ex."

"You knew they'd want you dead when you left him."

"I knew it was either let them kill me quickly or let him do it slowly by beating me down until I was a shell of myself. His people were all around me and they knew what was happening. They knew how he treated me. They saw the bruises and ignored them. I knew that my son would be at their mercy if I died, so I waited until he was 18 and knew the ways of their world before I walked out of the house and got in a cab to go and destroy the peace agreement between my dad and my father-in-law. Zacharia was an adult who'd just left for college and was living his life independent of his father's side of the family. I was content that I'd done everything I could to make him a good man. To make him the opposite of the other men in his family. I didn't have to work hard to turn him against them. He lived in the same house. He heard what went on and saw the aftermath of the violence his father inflicted on me and the damage it caused. When he'd try to lash out, I'd talk to him and tell him to hold onto it until he had a plan in place. He learned very early on how to keep a smile on his face while his brain was making a plan for when he took over."

"Holy shit."

"I wonder every day when my son will step up and fulfill his destiny. When I hear that my father-in-law is dead, I'll know that my son has decided it's his turn to run the family and that he's eradicated the problem. I have no doubt that my father-in-law will die a horrible death that has nothing to do with natural causes. Zacharia and my brothers are just biding their time."

"Fuck. That's intense. And terrifying, to be honest."

"That's life. Well, that's my old life."

"What other secrets do you have? Any more tricks up your sleeve?"

Paula laughed and shook her head. "Not up my sleeve, babe. Those aren't dependable. I do have this trick, though." I watched as she reached down into the neck of her shirt. I heard something rip, and when she pulled her hand out, a wire came with it. She kept tugging and the wire sprung free. She laid it down on the bar and reached back into her bra. I heard another tear, and she pulled out two of the razor rings the guys had been studying last night. She reached into her bra with the other hand and pulled out a sharp piece of plastic with two finger-sized holes on the end. "I keep my tricks in my bra, babe. I'm never without a good bra."

Paula put the rings on her index fingers, slid the middle and ring finger of her right hand into the holes at the bottom of the small, plastic knife so that it stuck up over her fingers, then wrapped ends of the wires around her hands a few times and pulled it taut in front of her.

She had razor blades, a knife, and a garrot in her fucking bra, and I'd never even known it.

"Have I told you today how much I love you and that I'll try my very hardest to never, *ever* piss you off?"

Paula laughed as she dropped her weapons onto the bar. She looked up at me and said, "I love you, too, Hook. It's hard for me to admit how much I love you because I'd always thought I'd have to leave. But I'm not going to leave you. Not unless you want me to. I'll stay here with you and fight if I have to, but I'm not going to run away and lose the chance you're giving me at a happy life."

I walked around the bar, pulled her into my arms, and kissed the top of her head. "I love every little part of your badass, even if you *could* kill me in nine different ways before I ever even knew you were pissed."

"I'd never hurt you on purpose, Hook."

"And I'd never hurt you, little one. I love you too much to even consider it."

We stood there together in the kitchen for a while, holding each other close. Suddenly, Paula laughed and leaned her head back so she could look at me. "The next time all the guys are together, I'm going to wow them with my brarmory. I want to see how many of them I can stun speechless."

"Your brarmory?"

"That's what my brother calls it. You think the guys will be shocked?"

"I think that if you did that little demonstration, even Preacher would be speechless for a while. That's one hell of a party trick."

"Let's go to the bedroom, and I'll show you a few other tricks I'm proud of, but these don't require any weapons."

"Oh, hell yeah. I'm all . . ."

Paula and I jumped when the front door flew open. I turned my head and saw Frankie, Jenn, Brea, and Sis walking through the door. Right behind them was Sin's girl Lyric and her best friend Kerrigan.

"We gave you all day with her. It's our turn," Jenn informed me as she grabbed Paula's arm and pulled her away. "Go do man shit while we catch up with our girl. She's got an adventure to tell us about, and that requires lots of liquor."

"I don't want to . . ."

"Hook. Go to Jenn's house. Sin and a few of his guys are already there with all the other convicts. It's time for Paula to spend a little time with her tribe and relax," Brea informed me. "Now, shoo! Run along little man. Our turn!"

"I brought duck tape!" Sis yelled from where she'd flopped down on the couch. "Mom actually made me sign an agreement that I wouldn't video shit."

"Oh my God." Paula laughed as she turned back around and tilted her head for a kiss. "Go play with the boys, big guy. I'll show you those tricks we talked about later tonight."

"I love you, little one."

"I love you too."

"I can't fucking believe you really have a pet tiger!"

"Did you think I'd been lying to you, Zacharia?"

"Technically, Tonya is still a wild animal. She just lives here in the house with us, and we do her bidding. She could kill us all if she set her mind to it," Hook reminded us from where he was standing at the pool table playing a game with my brother Vincente. "Tonya's a lot like your mom."

"Isn't that the fucking truth?" I heard my other brother, Antonio, agree from his spot on the couch where he had been talking with Pop.

"We're having dinner at Boss and Jenn's house tomorrow. Wait until you see her pets. It's like going to Old McDonald's farm."

"It would take a lot to top a tiger," Zacharia replied from the floor where he was rubbing Tonya's belly.

Tonya flopped around until her head was in Zacharia's lap, and he started stretching the underside of her neck, her sweet spot. She started huffing like she did when she was happy, and my son looked up at me as he laughed at the big cat.

For the first time in the eight years since I'd left my family, my brothers and my son had found a way to visit me together. They planned to stay for almost a week. It was an unscheduled visit, and I'd only found out about it as the three were boarding a plane on their way to Texas.

I knew something was fishy, but I didn't want to ask. I planned on enjoying their time with me however I could get it.

Just before we'd parked the car at the airport to pick them up, I'd gotten a call from Frankie. She was so excited that I could barely understand her. After she started talking, I could hardly breathe. I felt like my heart was beating out of my chest.

She'd heard from her brother that my ex-husband had been killed after falling while hiking with his girlfriend in the mountains of Italy. Search and rescue had to be called in to recover his body off the side of the mountain, and it was being flown back to the US for his funeral. The service wasn't scheduled yet because his father had been in a horrible car accident and wasn't expected to survive.

While I was reeling from that news, Frankie dropped another bomb that made me smile, but terrified me a little at the same time.

During the wreck, the car my ex-father-in-law was driving bounced around and flipped end over end. The gun he'd had stored in the glove compartment had gotten loose and discharged three times. All three shots had managed to hit him directly in the chest.

My son, the man currently playing with a tiger on my kitchen floor, was now the head of a prominent crime family. But true to form, he didn't let it go to his head. He was busy enjoying all the good things around him for now, just as I'd taught him when he was a child.

The fact that his father and grandfather had been killed, most likely on his own orders and with help from my two brothers, didn't seem to phase him at all. If anything, he seemed happier and lighter than I'd ever seen him.

Sometimes, life took a crazy turn you didn't expect, but if you were lucky, everything turned out okay in the end.

I looked over at Hook, and he winked at me. He knew how insane things could be, but he was enjoying the good that surrounded us. So was I.

THE END

COMING SOON

The Time Served MC is part of the Tenillo Guardians series together with the Ares Infidels MC written by Ciara St. James. Each series will stand alone, but Cee and Ciara have written their books in a way that will give the reader a perspective from each club as they work together.

The second book in the Ares Infidels MC series entitled Executioner's Enthrallment will be released by Ciara St. James on July 1, 2021, and it will follow the timeline of Cee's book that you just finished.

Executioner's years as a US Marine has made him a hard, dangerous man no one wants to cross. He uses that persona to carry out his job as enforcer for his club, the Ares Infidels.

While working with his brothers and an ally club, he visits a local business and has his world turned upside down. They've met before, but he had lost hope of ever finding her again. She's tried to forget him and what he made her feel.

He's incensed when he finds out the extortionists who targeted her family made darker threats toward her. He's determined she'll be his, and he'll do whatever it takes to make that happen and to keep her and her family safe.

Skye's life wasn't the best or easiest even before her dad left the family high and dry years ago. They battled daily to keep afloat. A chance meeting with him is the last thing she expected or wanted. He needs to realize that she's not looking for a relationship.

She's learned some hard life lessons that convinced her a happily ever after isn't in the cards for her. Skye keeps pushing him away while he keeps edging ever closer. However, Executioner isn't going to lose this fight. Even when she puts distance between them to protect her heart.

Something has to give, and it does. Her past comes to light, her present takes a crazy turn, and her future is looking like it might be the best thing to ever happen to her. If she can let go of her fear and pain, she'll forever be Executioner's Enthrallment.

You can find information about Ciara St. James and her books on www.ciarastjames.com.

About the Author

Cee Bowerman is proud, lifelong resident of Texas. She is married to her own long-haired, tattooed biker and is the proud mom to three mostly adult kids - a daughter and two sons. She believes in love, second chances, rescue dogs, and happily ever after.

Cee received her first romance novel along with a bag of other books from her granny when she was recovering from surgery at 15. She has been hooked on reading romances ever since. For years, she had a dream of writing her own series of stories, but motherhood and all the other grown up responsibilities kept getting in the way. Luckily, with the support of her family and the encouragement of her son, she purchased a computer and let her dreams become a reality.

Printed in Great Britain
by Amazon